DEBBIE MACOMBER

A Gift to Last

MIRA®

ISBN 1-55166-930-7

A GIFT TO LAST
Copyright © 2002 by MIRA Books.

CAN THIS BE CHRISTMAS?
Copyright © 1998 by Debbie Macomber.

SHIRLEY, GOODNESS AND MERCY
Copyright © 1999 by Debbie Macomber.

Visit us at www.mirabooks.com

Printed in U.S.A.

CONTENTS

CAN THIS BE CHRISTMAS?

For my dear friend Betty and her Judge
Many years of happiness, my friend
To the new
Mr. and Mrs. Jim Roper

One

"I'll Be Home for Christmas"

A robust version of "Little Drummer Boy" played in the background as Len Dawber glanced at his watch—for at least the tenth time in five minutes. He looked around the depot impatiently, hardly noticing the Christmas decorations on the windows and walls—the cardboard Santa's sleigh, the drooping garland and blinking lights.

Len was waiting with a herd of other holiday travelers to board the train that would take him to Boston. The snowstorm that had started last evening meant his early-morning flight out of Bangor, Maine, had been canceled and the airport closed. Although the airlines couldn't be blamed for the weather, they'd done everything possible to arrange transportation out of Maine. Len suspected more than a few strings had been pulled to get seats on the already full midmorning train. Maybe some of the original passengers canceled, he thought with faint hope.

Because, unfortunately, that crowded train was his only chance of making it to Boston in time to connect with his flight home for Christmas.

Len got to his feet, relinquishing his place on the hard station bench to a tired-looking man. He walked quickly to the door and stepped outside. He lifted his gaze toward the sky. Huge flakes of snow swirled in the wind, obscuring his view. His shoulder muscles tensed with frustration until he could no longer remain still. This was exactly what he'd feared would happen when he'd awakened that morning. Even then the clouds had been dark and ominous, threatening his plans and his dreams of a reunion with Amy.

Despite the snow that stung his eyes and dampened his hair, Len began to pace back and forth along the platform, peering down the tracks every few seconds. No train yet. Damn it! Stuck in New England on Christmas Eve.

This was supposed to be the season of joy, but there was little evidence of that in the faces around him. Most people were burdened with luggage and armfuls of Christmas packages. Some of the gift wrap was torn, the bows limp and tattered. The children, sensing their parents' anxiety, were cranky and restless. The younger ones whined and clung to their mothers.

Worry weighed on Len's heart. He *had* to catch the Boston flight, otherwise he wouldn't make it home to Rawhide, Texas, today. He'd miss his date with Amy and the family's Christmas Eve celebration. Part of his precious leave would be squandered because of the snowstorm.

There was another reason he yearned for home. Len didn't intend this to be an ordinary Christmas. No, this Christmas would be one of the best in his entire life. It had everything to do with Amy—and the engagement ring burning a hole in his uniform pocket.

Len had enlisted in the navy following high-school graduation and taken his submarine training in New London, Connecticut. Afterward, he'd been assigned to the sub base in Bangor, Maine. He thoroughly enjoyed life on the East Coast, so different from anything he'd known in Texas, and wondered if Amy would like it, too....

Len was proud to serve his country and seriously considered making the navy his career, but that decision depended on a number of things. Amy's answer, for one.

A real drawback of military life was this separation from his family. On his most recent trip home last September, he'd come to realize how much he loved Amy Brent. In the weeks since, he'd decided to ask her to marry him. They planned to be together that very night, Christmas Eve—the most wonderful night of the year. Once they were alone, away from family and friends, Len intended to propose.

He loved Amy; he had no doubts about that. He

wasn't a man who gave his heart easily, and he'd made sure, in his own mind at least, that marriage was what he truly wanted. In the weeks since their last meeting, he'd come to see that loving her was for real and for always.

They hadn't talked about marriage, not the way some couples did, but he was confident she loved him, too. He paused for a moment and held in a sigh as the doubts came at him, thick as the falling snow. Lately Len had noticed that Amy seemed less like her normal self. They hadn't talked much, not with him saving to buy the diamond. And it was difficult for Amy to call him at the base. So they'd exchanged letters—light newsy letters with little mention of feelings. He had to admit he found their letters enjoyable to read—and even to write—and the cost of stamps was a lot more manageable than some of his phone bills had been. The truth was, he couldn't afford to spend money on long-distance calls anymore, not the way he had in previous months. His airfare home hadn't been cheap, either.

It wasn't as if he'd put off traveling until the last minute, which Amy seemed to suspect. He'd been on duty until the wee hours of this morning; he'd explained all that in a letter he'd mailed earlier in the week, when he'd sent her his flight information. Although Amy hadn't come right out and said it, he knew she'd been disappointed he couldn't arrive earlier, but that was navy life.

He hadn't received a letter from her in ten days, which was unusual. Then again, perhaps not. After all, they'd be seeing each other soon. Amy and his parents were scheduled to pick him up in Dallas, and together they'd drive home to Rawhide. He closed his eyes and pictured their reunion, hoping the mental image would help calm his jangled nerves. It did soothe him, but not for long.

He had to get home for Christmas. He just had to.

This was Cathy Norris's first Christmas without Ron, and she refused to spend it in Maine. She'd buried her husband of forty-one years that October; her grief hadn't even begun to abate. The thought of waking up Christmas morning without him had prompted her to accept her daughter's invitation. She'd be joining Madeline and her young family in Boston for the holidays.

Cathy had postponed the decision until last week for a number of reasons. To begin with, she wasn't a good traveler and tended to stay close to home. Ron, on the other hand, had adored adventure and loved trekking through the woods and camping and fishing with his friends. Cathy was more of a homebody. She'd never flown or taken the train by herself before—but then, she was learning, now, to do a great many unfamiliar things on her own. In the past Ron had always been with her, seeing to their tickets, their luggage and any unforeseen problems. He had been such a dear husband, so thoughtful and generous.

The battle with cancer had been waged for a year. Ron had put up a gallant fight, but in the end he'd been ready to die, far more ready than she was to let him go. Trivial as it seemed now, she realized that subconsciously she'd wanted him to live until after the holidays.

Naturally she'd never said anything. How could she, when such a request was purely selfish? It wasn't as if Ron could choose when he would die. Nevertheless, she'd clung to him emotionally far longer than she should have—until she'd painfully acknowledged that her fears were denying her husband a peaceful exit from life. Then with an agony that had all but crippled her, she'd kissed him one final time. Holding his limp hand between her own, she'd sat by his bedside, loving him with her entire being, and waited until he'd breathed his last.

Ron's death clouded what would otherwise have been her favorite month of the year. She found it devastating to be around others celebrating the season while she struggled to shake her all-consuming grief. She'd accepted Madeline's invitation as part of a concerted effort to survive the season of peace and goodwill.

Charting a new course for herself at this age was more of a challenge than she wanted. Life, however, had seen fit to make her a widow one month, then thrust her into the holiday season the next.

She was doing her best, trying to cope with her grief, finding the courage to smile now and again for her children's sake. They realized how difficult the holidays were for her of course, but her daughters were grieving, too.

This snowstorm had been an unwelcome hitch in her careful plans. Madeline had urged her to come sooner, but Cathy had foolishly resisted, not wanting to overstay her welcome. She'd agreed to visit until the twenty-seventh. Ron had always said that company, like fish, began to smell after three days.

"Mom," Madeline had said when she'd phoned early that morning, "I heard on the news there's a huge snowstorm headed your way."

"I'm afraid it arrived last night." The wind had moaned audibly outside her window as she spoke.

"What are you going to do?" Madeline, her youngest, tended to worry; unfortunately she'd inherited that trait from her mother.

"Do?" Cathy repeated as if a fierce winter blizzard was of little concern. "I'm taking the train to Boston to join you, Brian and the children for Christmas. What else is there to do?"

"But how will you get to the station?"

Cathy had already worked that out. "I've phoned for a taxi."

"But, Mom—"

"I'm sure everything will be fine," Cathy said firmly, hoping she sounded confident even though she was an emotional wreck. She felt as though her life was caving in around her. Stuck in Bangor over Christmas, grieving for Ron—that would have been more than Cathy could handle. If spending the holiday with family meant taking her chances in the middle of a snowstorm, then so be it.

The first hurdle had been successfully breached. Listening to Andy Williams crooning a Christmas ballad, Cathy stood in line at the Bangor train depot, along with half the town, it seemed. The taxi fare had been exorbitant, but at least she was here, safe and sound. She'd packed light, leaving plenty of room in her suitcase for gifts for her two youngest granddaughters. Shopping had been a chore this year, so she'd decided simply to give Madeline and Brian a check and leave it at that, but she couldn't give money to her grandchildren. They were much too young for that. The best gifts she could think to bring them were books, plus a toy each.

Madeline had consented to let Lindsay and Angela, aged three and five, open their presents that evening following church services. Then the children could climb onto Cathy's lap and she'd read them to sleep. The thought of holding her grandchildren close helped ease the ache in her heart.

Everything would be all right now that she was at the depot, she reassured herself. Soon she'd be with her family. The train might be late, but it would get there eventually.

All her worries had been for nothing.

Matthew McHugh hated Christmas. And he didn't have a problem expressing that opinion. As for the season of goodwill—what a laugh. Especially now, when he was stuck in an overcrowded train depot, waiting for the next train to Boston where he'd catch the flight into LAX. The timing of this snowstorm had been impeccable. Every seat in the station was taken, and people who weren't sitting nervously paced the confined area, waiting for the train, which was already fifteen minutes late. Some, like that guy in the navy uniform, were even prowling the platform—as though *that* would make the train come any faster.

Christmas Eve, and the airports, train depots and bus stations were jammed. Everyone was in a rush to get somewhere, him included. As a sales rep for a Los Angeles-based software company, Matt was a seasoned traveler. And he figured anyone who spent a lot of time in airports would agree: Christmas was the worst. Crying babies, little old ladies, cranky kids—he'd endured it all. Most of it with ill grace.

His boss, Ruth Shroeder, who'd been promoted over him, had handed him this assignment early in the week. She'd purposely sent him to the other side of the country just so he'd know *she* was in charge.

Rub his face in it, so to speak. This could easily have been a wasted trip; no one bought computer software three days before Christmas. Fortunately he'd outfoxed her and made the sale. By rights, he should be celebrating, but he experienced little satisfaction and no sense of triumph.

Ruth had been expecting him to make a fuss, demand that the assignment go to one of the junior sales reps. Matt had merely smiled and reached for the plane tickets. He'd sold the software, but was left feeling that although he'd won the battle, he was destined to lose the war.

And a whole lot more.

Pam, his wife of fifteen years, hadn't been the least bit understanding about this trip. If ever he'd needed her support it was now, but all she'd done was add to his burden. "Christmas, Matt? You're leaving three days before Christmas?"

What irritated him most was her complete and total lack of appreciation for his feelings. It wasn't like he'd *asked* for this trip or wanted to be away from the family. The fact that Pam had chosen the evening of his departure to start an argument revealed how little she recognized the stress he'd been under since the promotions were announced.

"I already said it couldn't be helped," he'd explained calmly as he packed his bag. His words were devoid of emotion, although plenty of it simmered just below the surface. He carefully placed an extra shirt in his bag.

Pam had gone strangely quiet.

"I'll be home Christmas Eve in time for dinner," he'd promised, not meeting her eyes. "My flight gets into LAX at four, so I'll be back here by six." He spoke briskly, reassuringly.

Silence.

"Come on, Pam, you have to know I don't like this any better than you do," he said, and forcefully jerked the zipper on his garment bag closed.

"You're going to miss Jimmy in the school play."

He was sorry about that, but there were worse things in life than not seeing his six-year-old son as an elf. "I've already talked to him about it, and Jimmy understands." Even if his wife didn't.

"What was he supposed to say?" Pam demanded.

Matt's shrug was philosophical.

"You were away when Rachel had the lead in the Sunday-school program, too."

Matt frowned, trying to remember missing that. "Rachel was in a Sunday-school program?"

"Three years ago... I see you've already forgotten. It broke her heart, but I notice you've conveniently let it slip your mind."

Matt had heard enough. He folded his garment bag over his arm and reached for his coat and briefcase.

"You don't have anything else to say?" Pam cried as she stormed after him.

"So you can shovel more guilt at me? Do you want me to confess I'm a rotten father? Okay, fine." His voice gained volume. "Matthew McHugh is a rotten father."

Pam blinked back tears. Matt longed to hold her, but they'd gone too far for that.

"You aren't a bad father," she said after a moment, and his heart softened. A fight now was the last thing either of them needed. He was about to tell her so when she continued. "It's as a husband that you've completely failed."

Matt swore under his breath. Any tenderness he'd felt earlier shattered.

"You're leaving me to deal with Christmas, the shopping, dinners, everything. I can't take it anymore."

"Take it?" he shouted. "Do you know how many women would love to be able to stay home with their families? You have it easy compared to working mothers who're out there competing in a man's world. If you think shopping and cooking dinner is too much for you, then—"

Pam's expression grew mutinous. "My not working was a decision we made together! I can't believe you're throwing that in my face now. If you're saying you want me to get a job, fine, consider it done."

Matt's fist tightened around his briefcase handle. That wasn't what he wanted, and Pam knew it.

"All I'm saying is I could use a little support."

"It wouldn't hurt you to support me, either," she snapped.

They glared at each other, neither willing to give in.

"Have a good time," she said flippantly. "Just go. I'll do what I always do and make excuses for you with the children and your parents. I'll be at the school for Jimmy, so don't worry—not that you ever have."

If Matt heard about this stupid Christmas pageant one more time, he'd blow a fuse. Rather than continue the argument, he headed out the door. "I'll call you in the morning."

"Don't bother," she exploded, and slammed the door in his wake.

Matt had taken his wife at her word and hadn't phoned once in the past three days. It was the first time in fifteen years on the road that he hadn't called his family. Pam had the number of his hotel, and she hadn't made the effort to call him, either. They'd argued before, all couples did, but they'd never allowed a disagreement to go on this long.

Now as he stood in the crowded depot, waiting for the train to arrive, Matt was both tired and bored. For a man who'd purposely avoided any contact with his wife, he was in an all-fired hurry to get home.

This should be the happiest Christmas of Kelly Berry's life. After a ten-year struggle she and Nick were first-time parents. She liked to joke that her labor had lasted five years. That was how long they'd been on the adoption waiting list. Five years, two months and seventeen days, to be exact. Then the call had finally come, and twenty hours later they'd brought their daughter home from the hospital.

In less than a day, their entire existence had been turned upside down. After the long frustrating years of waiting, they were parents at last.

This would be their first trip home to Macon, Georgia, since they'd signed the adoption papers. Brittany Ann Berry's grandparents were eager to meet her.

The infant fussed in her arms and let loose with a piercing cry that cut into Neil Diamond's rendition of "Jingle Bells." A businessman scowled at them; Nick, muttering under his breath, grabbed the diaper bag. Doing the best she could, Kelly gently placed the baby over her shoulder and rubbed her tiny back.

"She's all right," Kelly said, smiling to reassure her husband while he rummaged through the diaper bag in search of the pacifier.

As Nick sat upright, he dragged one hand down his face, already showing signs of stress. They hadn't so much as left the train depot and already their nerves were shot. Despite their eagerness to be parents, the adjustment was a difficult one. Nick had proved to be a nervous father. Kelly wasn't all that adept at parenthood herself. She smiled again at Nick, accepting the pacifier. Everything would be easier once Brittany slept through the night, she was sure of that.

Her two older sisters were much better at this mothering business than she was. Never had Kelly missed her family more; never had the need to talk out her fears and doubts been more pressing.

This flight home was an extravagance Nick and Kelly could ill afford. Then the storm had blown in, with all its complications, and they'd been rerouted to Boston by train.

A whistle sang from the distance, and the sound of it was as beautiful as church bells.

The train was coming, just like the man at the ticket counter had promised. She listened to the announcement listing the destinations between here and Boston as people stood and reached for their bags. Nick automatically started gathering the baby paraphernalia.

They were headed home, each and every one of them. A little snow wasn't going to stand in their way.

Two

"I Wonder as I Wander"

The train filled up quickly, and Len was fortunate to find a seat next to a grandmotherly woman who pulled out her knitting the moment she'd made herself comfortable. Mesmerized, he watched her fingers expertly weave the yarn, mentally counting stitches in an effort to keep his mind off the time and how long it was taking his fellow passengers to get settled.

The nervousness in the pit of his stomach began to ease as the conductor, an elderly white-haired gentleman, shuffled slowly down the aisle, checking tickets.

"Will we reach Boston before noon?" That question came from the woman with the baby seated across from him.

Len was grateful she'd asked; he was looking for answers himself.

"Hard to say with the snow and all."

"But it has to," she groaned, again voicing his own concerns. "We'll never catch our flight otherwise."

"I heard the airports are closed between Bangor and Boston," he said amiably. He scratched the side of his white head as if that would aid his concentration. "The train's running, though, and you can rest assured we'll do our best to see you make it to Boston in time."

His words reassured more than the young couple with the baby. Len's anxious heart rested a little easier, too. Glancing at the older woman in the seat next to him, he decided some conversation might help distract him.

"Are you catching a flight in Boston?"

"Oh, no," she said, tugging on the red yarn. "My daughter and her family live in Boston. I'm joining them for Christmas. Where are you headed?"

"Rawhide, Texas," Len said, letting his pride in his state show through his words.

"Texas," she repeated, not missing a stitch. "Ron and I visited Texas once. Ron wanted to see the Alamo. He's my husband…was my husband. He died this October."

"I'm sorry."

"So am I," she murmured with such utter sadness that Len had to look away. She recovered quickly and continued. "It's mind-boggling that people can fly across this country in only a few hours, isn't it?"

It was a fact that impressed Len, too, but he was more grateful than astonished. He felt even more appreciative when the whistle pierced the chatter going on about him. Almost immediately the train started to move, then quickly gained speed. Everyone aboard seemed to give a collective sigh of relief.

Len and the widow chatted amicably for several minutes and eventually exchanged names. Cathy asked him a couple of questions, about Texas and the navy, and he asked her a few. After a while, their conversation died down and they returned to their own thoughts.

The train traveled at a slow but steady pace for an hour or so. The unrelenting snow whirled around them, but the passengers were warm and cozy. For all the worry this storm had caused earlier, it didn't seem nearly as intimidating from inside the train. Relaxed, Len stretched out his legs, confident that with a little luck, he'd connect with the flight out of Logan International.

The train stopped now and then at depots on the way. Each stop resulted in a quick exchange of passengers. Len noticed that the storm appeared to have changed people's holiday plans; far more exited the train than entered. The brief stops lasted no more than ten minutes, and soon there were a number of vacant seats in the passenger car. Before long Len heard the conductor say they'd be crossing into New Hampshire.

Len figured you could fit all of these tiny New England states inside Texas. He'd seen cattle ranches that were larger than Rhode Island! The thought produced a pang of homesickness. The song sure got it right—there's no place like home for the holidays. His life belonged to the navy now, but he was a Texas boy through and through.

"Do you have someone at home waiting for you?" Cathy asked him.

"My family," Len told her, and added, prematurely, "and my fiancée." Saying the words produced a happiness in him that refused to be squelched.

"How nice for you."

"Very nice," he said. Then thinking it might help ease his mind, he opened the side zipper of his carry-on bag and pulled out Amy's most recent letter, dated two weeks earlier.

Dear Len,
I waited until ten for you to phone, then realized it was eleven your time and you probably wouldn't be calling. I was feeling low about it, then received your letter this afternoon. I'm glad you decided to write. You say you're not good at writing letters, but I disagree. This one was very sweet. It's nice to have something to hold in my hand, that I can read again and again, unlike a telephone conversation. While it's always good to hear the sound of your voice, when we hang up, there's nothing left.

Everything's going along fine here at home and at work. For all my complaining about not finding a more glamorous job, I've discovered I actually enjoy being part of the nursing-home staff. The travel agency that didn't hire me is the one to lose out.

Did I tell you we had quite a stir last week? Mr. Perkins exposed himself in the middle of a pinochle game. All the ladies were outraged, but I noticed that the sign-up sheet for pinochle this Thursday is full. Mrs. MacPherson lost her teeth, but they were eventually found. (You don't want to know where.) I still have my lunch in Mr. Danbar's room; he seems to enjoy my company, although he hasn't spoken a word in three years. I chatter away and tell him all about you and me and how excited I am that you're coming home for Christmas.

I was pleased that your mother asked me if I wanted to tag along when she and your dad pick you up at the airport on Christmas Eve. I'll be there, you know I will—which brings me to something else. Something I've been wanting to ask you for a long time.

Do you remember my joke about sailors having a woman in every port? You laughed and reminded me that, as a submariner, you didn't see that many ports above water. Bangor's a long way from Rawhide, though, isn't it? I guess I'm asking you about other women.

Well, I'd better close for now. I'll see you in two weeks and we can talk more then.

Love,
Amy

Len folded the letter and slipped it back inside the envelope. Amy shouldn't need to ask him about other women. He didn't know what had made her so insecure, but he'd noticed the doubt in her voice ever since he returned in September.

The diamond ring should relieve her worries. He smiled just thinking about it. He could hardly wait to see the look on her face.

Cathy set her knitting aside and stared sightlessly out the train window. The snow obliterated everything, not that the scenery interested her. Try as she might, she couldn't stop thinking about Ron.

Other years, she'd been working in her kitchen Christmas Eve day, baking cookies and pies, getting ready for the children and grandchildren to arrive. As a surprise—although it had long since ceased to be one—she'd always baked Ron a lemon meringue pie, his favorite. And he'd always pretend he was stunned that she'd go to all that trouble just for him.

Christmas had been the holiday her husband loved most. He was like a kid, decorating the outside of the house with strand upon strand of colorful lights. Last year he'd outdone all his previous efforts, as if he'd known even then that he wouldn't be here this Christmas.

She remembered how, every year, Ron had wanted to put up the tree right after Thanksgiving. She was lucky if she could hold him off until it was officially December.

It took them an entire day to decorate the tree. Not that they ever chose such a large one. Trimming their Christmas tree was a ritual that involved telling each other stories about past Christmases, recalling where each decoration came from—whether it was made by one of the girls or bought on vacation somewhere or given to them by a friend. It wasn't just ornaments, baubles of glass and wood and yarn, that hung from the evergreen branches but memories. They still had several from when they were first married, back in 1957. And about ten years ago, Cathy had cross-stitched small frame ornaments with pictures of everyone in the family. It'd taken her months and Ron was as proud of those tiny frames as if he'd done the work himself.

Memories… Cathy couldn't face them this Christmas. All she could do was hope they brought her comfort in the uncertain future.

Since he'd retired from the local telephone company four years ago, Ron had used his spare time puttering around his wood shop, building toys for the grandchildren. Troy and Peter had been thrilled with the race cars he'd fashioned from blocks of wood.

Ron had taken such pride in those small cars. Angela and Lindsay had adored the dollhouse he'd carefully designed and built for them. The end table he'd started for Cathy remained in his wood shop unfinished. He'd longed to complete it, but the chemotherapy had drained away his strength, and in the months that followed, it was enough for him just to make it through the day.

Ron wouldn't be pleased with her, Cathy mused. She'd made only a token effort to decorate this year. No tree, no lights on the house. She'd set out a few things—a crèche on the fireplace mantel and the two cotton snowmen Madeline had made as a craft project years ago when she was in Girl Scouts.

Actually Cathy couldn't see the point of doing more. Not when it hurt so much. And not when she'd be leaving, anyway. She did manage to bake Madeline's favorite shortbread cookies, but that had been the only real baking she'd done.

Resting her head against the seat, Cathy closed her eyes. She tried to let the sound of the train lull her to sleep, but memories refused to leave her alone, flashing through her mind in quick succession. The sights and sounds of the holidays in happier times. Large family dinners, the house filled with the scents of mincemeat pies and sage dressing. Music, too; there was always plenty of music.

Madeline played the piano and Gloria, their oldest, had been gifted with a wonderful voice. Father and daughter had sung Christmas carols together, their voices blending beautifully. At least one of their three daughters had made it home for the holidays every year. But Gloria couldn't afford the airfare so soon after the funeral, and Jeannie was living in New York now and it was hard for her to take time off from her job, especially when she'd already asked for two weeks in order to be with her father at the end. Madeline would have come, Cathy guessed, if she'd asked, but she'd never do that.

Dear God, she prayed, *just get me through the next three days.*

Matthew McHugh's patience was shot. The cranky baby from the station was in the same car and hadn't stopped fussing yet. Matthew's head throbbed with the beginnings of a killer headache. His argument with Pam played over and over in his mind until it was so distorted he didn't know what to think anymore.

If Pam was upset about his being gone this close to Christmas, he could only imagine what she'd say when he arrived home hours later than scheduled.

He could picture it now. His parents, Pam and the kids, all waiting for him to pull into the driveway so they could eat dinner. When he did walk in the house, they'd glare at him as though he'd stayed away just to inconvenience them. He'd seen it happen before.

As though he were somehow personally responsible for weather conditions and canceled flights.

As for Pam's complaining about having to do all the shopping and cooking herself, he didn't understand it. If she preferred, they could order one of those take-out Christmas dinners from the local diner. She didn't need to do all this work if she didn't want to. The choice was hers. He couldn't care less if the jellied salad was homemade or came out of a container. Pam was putting pressure on herself.

The same thing applied to inviting his parents for Christmas Eve dinner. He wasn't the one who'd asked them. That had been Pam's doing. His mom and dad lived less than an hour away; they could stop by the house any time they wanted. To make a big deal out of having a meal together on Christmas Eve was ridiculous to him, especially if Pam was going to bitch about it.

The baby cried again. Matt clenched his fists and tried to hold on to his patience. The infant wasn't the only irritation, either. A little girl, five or so, was standing on the seat in front of his, staring at him.

"What's your name?" she asked.

"Scrooge."

"My name's Kate."

"Shouldn't you be sitting down, Kate?" he asked pointedly, hoping the kid's mother heard him and took action. She didn't.

"It's going to be Christmas tomorrow," she said, ignoring his question.

"So I hear." He attempted to look busy, too busy to be bothered.

The kid didn't take the hint.

"Santa Claus is coming to Grandma's house."

"Wonderful." His voice was thick with sarcasm. "Don't you know it's impolite to stare?"

"No." The kid flashed him an easy smile. "I can read."

"Good for you."

"Do you want me to read you *How the Grinch Stole Christmas*? It's my favorite book."

"No."

An elderly black couple sat across the aisle from him. The woman scowled disapprovingly, her censure at his attitude toward the kid obvious. "Why don't you read to her?" Matt suggested, motioning to the woman. "I've got work to do."

"You're working?" shrieked Kate-the-pest.

"Yes," came his curt reply, "or trying to." He couldn't get any blunter than that.

"Can I read you my story?" Kate asked the biddy across the aisle from him. Matt flashed the old woman a grin. Served her right. Let *her* deal with the kid. All Matt wanted was a few moments' peace and quiet while he mulled over what was going to happen once he got home.

Some kind of commotion went on in front of him.

The little girl whimpered, and he felt a sense of right-eousness. Kate's mother had apparently put her foot down when the kid tried to climb out of her seat. Good, now maybe she'd leave him and everyone else alone. If he'd been smart he would have pretended he was asleep like the man sitting next to him.

"Mom said I have to stay in my seat," Kate said, tears glistening as she peered over the cushion at him. All he could see was her watery blue eyes and the top of her head with a fancy red bow.

Matt ignored her.

"Santa's going to bring me a—"

"Listen, kid, I don't care what Santa's bringing you. I've got work to do and I don't have time to chat with you. Now kindly turn around and stop bothering me."

Kate frowned at him, then plunked herself back in her seat and started crying.

Several people condemned him with their eyes, not that it concerned Matt. If they wanted to entertain the kid, fine, but he wanted no part of it. He had more important things on his mind than what Santa was bringing a spoiled little brat with no manners.

The train had been stopped for about five minutes. "Where are we now?" Kelly asked, gently rocking Brittany in her arms. The baby had fussed the entire time they'd been on the train. Nothing Kelly did calmed her. She wasn't hungry; her diaper was clean.

Kelly wondered if she might be teething. A mother was supposed to know these things, but Kelly could only speculate.

It helped that the train was becoming less crowded. With the storm, people seemed to be short-tempered and impatient. The guy who looked like a salesman was the worst; in fact, he was downright rude. She felt sorry for Kate and her mother. Kelly appreciated what it must be like traveling alone with a youngster. She'd never be able to do this without Nick. Frankly, she didn't know how anyone could travel with a baby and no one to help. An infant required so much *stuff*. It took hours just to organize and pack it all.

"According to the sign, we're in Abbott, New Hampshire," Nick informed her.

Kelly glanced out the window, through the still-falling snow. "Oh, Nick, look! This is one of those old-fashioned stations." The redbrick depot had a raised platform with several benches tucked protectively against the side, shielded from the snow by the roof's overhang. A ticket window faced the tracks and another window with many small panes looked into the waiting room.

"Hmm," Nick said, not showing any real interest.

"It's so quaint."

He didn't comment.

"I didn't know they had any of these depots left anymore. Do you think we could get off and look around a bit?"

She captured his attention with that. "You're joking, right?"

"We wouldn't have to take everything with us."

"The baby shouldn't be out in the cold."

Her enthusiasm faded. "Of course…she shouldn't."

The conductor walked down the center aisle and nodded pleasantly in Kelly's direction.

"That's a lovely old depot," she said.

"One of the last original stations in Rutherford County," he said with a glint of pride. "Built around 1880. Real pretty inside, too, with a potbellied stove and hardwood benches. They don't make 'em like this anymore."

"They sure don't," Kelly said, smiling.

"Shouldn't we be pulling out soon?" the man in the navy uniform asked, glancing at his watch.

"Anytime now," the conductor promised. "Nothing to worry about on this fine day. Snow or no snow, we're going to get you folks to Boston."

Three

"Have Yourself a Merry Little Christmas"

"It's been twenty minutes," Len said, straining to see what had caused the delay. Cupping his face with his hands, he pressed against the window and squinted at the station. The snow had grown heavier and nearly obliterated the building from view. The train had been sitting outside the depot in Abbott twice as long as it had at any previous stop. Apparently the powers-that-be didn't fully grasp the time constraints he and several other passengers were under to reach Logan International. Too much was at stake if he missed his flight.

"I'm sure everything will be all right," Cathy assured him, but he noticed that she was knitting at a frantic pace. She jerked hard on the yarn a couple of times, then had to stop and rework stitches, apparently because of a mistake.

Len saw that he wasn't the only one who seemed concerned. The cranky businessman got out of his seat and walked to the end of the compartment. He leaned over to peer out the window at the rear of the train car, as if that would tell him something he didn't already know.

"Someone's coming," he announced in a voice that said he wasn't going to be easily pacified. He wanted answers, and so did Len. Under normal circumstances Len was a patient man, but this was Christmas Eve and he had an engagement ring in his pocket.

The wind howled and snow blew into the compartment as the elderly conductor opened the door. He stepped quickly inside, then made his way to the front. "Folks, if I could have your attention a moment..."

Even before the man spoke, Len's gut told him it wasn't good news.

"We've got a problem on the line ahead."

"What kind of problem?" the sales rep demanded.

"Track's out."

A chorus of mumbles and raised voices followed.

The conductor raised his hands and the passengers fell silent. "We're doing the best we can."

"How long will it take to get it fixed?" The shout came from a long-haired guy at the front of the car. With his leather headband and fringed jacket, he resembled an overgrown hippie. He sat with a woman whose appearance complemented his—straight center-parted hair that reached the middle of her back and a long flower-sprigged dress under her heavy coat.

The conductor's face revealed doubt. "Couple of hours, possibly longer. Can't really say for sure."

"Hours!" Len exploded.

"We have a plane to catch," the young father cried, his anger spilling into outrage.

"The airlines arranged for us to be on the train for *this?*" the businessman shouted, not bothering to disguise his disgust. "We were better off waiting out the storm in Bangor."

"I'm sorry, but—"

"Does this podunk town have a car-rental agency?" someone asked. Len couldn't see who.

"Not right here. There's one in town, but with the storm, I'd strongly recommend none of you…"

Len didn't stick around to hear the rest. As best he could figure, he was less than sixty miles from Boston. If he could rent a car, there was a chance he might still make it to the airport on time. Moving faster than he would've thought possible, Len reached for his bag and raced off the train.

The moment he jumped onto the depot platform, a sudden blast of cold jolted him. He hunched his shoulders and kept his face down as he struggled against the icy wind to open the door. Not surprisingly, the inside of the depot was as quaint as the outside, with long rows of hardwood benches and a potbellied stove.

The stationmaster looked up as people started to flood inside. Apparently he handled the sale of tickets and whatever was available to buy—a few snack items, magazines, postcards and such. Three phones were positioned against the far wall. One bore an Out of Order sign.

A long, straggling line had already formed in front of the two working phones. Len counted ten people ahead of him and figured he had a fair chance of getting a vehicle until he remembered a friend telling him you needed to be twenty-five to rent one. His hopes sagged yet again. He was a year too young. Discouraged, he dropped out of line.

His nerves twisting, he sat on a hard wooden bench away from the others. It was hopeless. Useless to try. Even if the train had arrived anywhere close to its scheduled time, there was no guarantee he'd actually have a seat on the plane. Because of the storm, the airline had tried to get him on another flight leaving four hours later. But he was flying standby, which meant the only way he would get on board was if someone didn't show.

The reservation clerk had been understanding and claimed it wasn't as unlikely as it sounded. According to her, there were generally one or two seats available and he was at the top of the list. It had all sounded promising—and now this.

Cathy Norris sat down on the bench next to him. "I guess I should call my daughter," she said.

Len didn't know if she was speaking to him or not. "I suppose I should phone home, too."

The line for the phones had dwindled to five people. Len rejoined the group and impatiently waited his turn. It seemed to take forever before he was finally able to use the phone. He thought about contacting his parents, but he'd already spoken to them once that day.

Placing the charges on a calling card, he dialed Amy's number and prayed she was at home.

"Hello."

His relief at the sound of her soft drawl was enough to make him want to weep. "Hello, Amy Sue."

"Len?" Her voice rose with happy excitement. "Where are you?" Not giving him time to answer, she continued, "Your mother phoned earlier and said your flight had been canceled. Are you in Boston?"

"Abbott, New Hampshire."

"New Hampshire? Len, for mercy's sake, what are you doing there?"

"I wish I knew. The airline put us on a train."

"Your mother told me about the storm and how they closed the airport and everything," she said. He was distracted by the people lining up behind him, but her voice sounded…sad, almost as if she knew in advance what he was about to tell her.

"There's something wrong with the tracks. It's going to take a couple of hours to repair, so there's no telling what time I'll get to Boston."

"Oh, Len." Her voice was more breath than sound. "You're not going to make it home for Christmas, are you?"

He opened his mouth to insist otherwise, but the truth was, he no longer knew. "I want to, but..."

He could feel Amy's disappointment vibrate through the telephone wire. It was agony to be so far away and not able to hold her. "I'll do whatever I can to get to the airport on time, but there's no guarantee. You know I'd do anything to be with you right now, don't you?"

She didn't answer.

"Amy?" Talking with a lineup of people waiting to use the phone was a little inhibiting.

"I'll get in touch with your parents and let them know," she whispered, and her voice broke.

"I'll call you as soon as I hear anything," he said. Then, despite a dozen people eavesdropping on his conversation, he added, "I love you, Amy."

Unfortunately the line was already dead.

He should phone home, Matt decided, and even waited his turn in the long line that formed outside the telephone booth. He was three people away when he suddenly changed his mind. He had no idea why; then again, maybe he did.

It went without saying that Pam would be furious. He could hear her lambaste him now, and frankly, he wasn't in the mood for it.

He crossed to one of the vacant benches and sat down. These old seats might look picturesque, but they were a far sight from being comfortable. He shifted his position a number of times, crossed and uncrossed his legs.

As bad luck would have it, the couple with the baby sat directly opposite him. Matt didn't understand it. He seemed to attract the very people who irritated him most. Thankfully the infant was peacefully asleep in her mother's arms.

Matt studied the baby, remembering his own children at that age and how happy he and Pam had been in the early years of their marriage. That time seemed distant now. His dissatisfaction with his job didn't help. He felt as if he was struggling against everything that should make life good—his family, his marriage, his work. As if he stood waist-deep in the middle of a fast-flowing stream, fighting the current.

His wife had no comprehension of the stress he experienced day in and day out. According to her, he went out of his way to make her life miserable. Lately all she did was complain. If he went on the road, she complained; if he was home, she found fault with that, too.

The thought had come to him more than once these past few days that maybe they'd be better off living apart. He hadn't voiced it, but it was there in the back of his mind. Unhappy as she was, Pam must be entertaining these same thoughts. He couldn't remember the last time they'd honestly enjoyed each other's company.

Restless now, he stood and walked about. The depot had filled up, and there wasn't room enough for everyone to sit. The stationmaster was on the phone, and Matt watched the old man's facial expressions, hoping to get a hint of what was happening.

The man removed his black hat, frowned, then nodded. Matt couldn't read anything into that. He waited until the old guy had replaced the receiver. No announcement. Apparently there wasn't anything new to report. Matt checked his watch and groaned.

Thinking he might be more comfortable back on the train, he hurried outside, rushing through the bone-chilling wind and snow to the security of the train itself. The conductor and other staff had disappeared, Matt didn't know where. Probably all snug in the comfort of some friend's home. Not so for the passengers. The wind and snow nearly blinded him. He wasn't on board more than twenty minutes when the young father hurried inside and reached for a diaper bag tucked under the seat.

''Your first kid?'' Matt asked, bored and miserable. A few minutes of conversation might help pass the time. The answer was fairly obvious. He was no expert when it came to infants, but it was clear to him that this couple was far too high-strung about parenthood. To his way of thinking, once these two relaxed, their baby would, too.

The man nodded, then sat down abruptly. ''I had no idea it would be like this.''

''Nothing's the same after you have kids,'' Matt said. The train, now that it'd shut down, wasn't heated, and the piercing cold had quickly permeated the interior.

''Do you have kids?''

''Two,'' Matt said, and despite his mood, he grinned. ''Matt McHugh.'' He held out his hand.

''Nick Berry.''

''This isn't exactly how I expected to spend Christmas Eve.''

''Me, neither,'' Nick said. He lifted his shoulders and rubbed his bare hands. ''If it was up to me, we'd never have left Bangor, but Kelly's parents haven't seen the baby yet.''

Matt grunted in understanding.

''I'd better get back inside,'' Nick said. ''Kelly's waiting.''

''I might as well go in with you.'' It was obvious that he wouldn't be able to stay on the train much longer. He'd come for peace and quiet and found it not worth the price of having to sit alone in the cold. The temperature wasn't the only source of discomfort; he didn't like the turn his thoughts had taken. He didn't want a divorce, but he could see that was the direction he and Pam were headed.

Matt and Nick sprinted back into the depot just as

the stationmaster walked to the center of the room. Nick rejoined his wife and handed her the diaper bag.

"Folks," the old man said, raising his arms to attract their attention. "My name's Clayton Kemper and I'm here to give you as much information as I can about the situation."

"How much longer is this going to take?" the long-haired guy demanded.

"Yeah," someone else shouted. "When do we get out of here?"

"Now, folks, that's something I can't predict. The problem involves more than the storm. The tracks are out."

His words were followed by low dissatisfied murmurs.

"I realize you're anxious to be on your way, seeing it's Christmas Eve and all. But no one can tell us just how long it'll be before the repairs are finished. Our first estimate was two hours, but the repair crew ran into difficulties."

The murmurs rose in volume. "We need answers," Matt said loudly, his fists clenched. "Some of us are booked on flights."

Clayton Kemper held up his hands. "I'm sorry, folks, I really am, but like I said before, there's just no way of predicting this sort of thing. It could be another hour…or it could be till morning."

"Morning!" The grumbling erupted into a flurry of angry shouts.

"What about hotel rooms?" an older man asked, placing a protective arm around the woman beside him.

Matt watched Nick glance at his wife as he stepped forward. "That's a good question. Should we think about getting a hotel room?" It went without saying that a young family would be far more comfortable in one. "And what's available here?"

"There's a hotel in town and a couple of motels that should have a few rooms left. I can call and they'll send their shuttle vans for anyone who wants to be picked up. Same goes for the car rental agency. But—" Mr. Kemper rubbed the side of his jaw "—I can't tell you what would be best. When the repairs are finished, the train's pulling out. We won't have time to call all over town and round people up. If you're here, you go. If not, you'll need to wait for the next train."

Matt weighed his options and decided to wait it out. He was probably being too optimistic, but he'd rather take his chances at the depot. His choice wasn't the popular one. The majority of those on the train decided to get hotel rooms. Within ten minutes, the depot had emptied, leaving twenty or so hardy souls willing to brave the rest of the afternoon.

"What about you two?" Matt asked Nick, glancing at the younger man's wife and baby. He'd expected Nick to be among the first to seek more comfortable accommodations.

"Kelly thinks we should stay."

"It could be a long hard afternoon," Matt felt obliged to remind him. Later, when Nick and his wife changed their minds, there likely wouldn't be any rooms left. But that was none of his affair.

Matt's gaze went to the telephones. He probably should phone Pam, but the prospect brought him no pleasure. He'd wait until he had a few more pertinent details. No use upsetting her this soon. She had four hours yet before she needed to know he wasn't on his scheduled flight. In this instance ignorance was bliss.

"Mother…oh dear, this isn't working out the way I'd hoped." Madeline's distress rang over the wire.

Cathy's thoughts echoed her daughter. She pressed the telephone to her ear. "I don't want you to worry."

"I have every right to worry," Madeline snapped. "I should have come up there and gotten you myself."

"Nonsense." As far as Cathy was concerned, that would only have made matters worse. The last thing she wanted was to take her daughter away from her family on Christmas Eve.

"But Daddy would—" Madeline abruptly cut off the rest of what she was about to say.

"I'm perfectly fine."

"You're in the middle of a snowstorm on Christmas Eve. You're stuck without family, alone in some train depot in a dinky town in New Hampshire. You are not fine, Mother.''

Alone. The word leaped out of her daughter's mouth and hit Cathy hard. Hard enough that she took an involuntary step backward. Alone. That was how she'd felt since Ron's death. It seemed as though she wandered from day to day without purpose, linked to no one, lost, confused. And consumed by a grief so painful it virtually incapacitated her. All she had was the promise that time would eventually ease this ache in her heart.

''The entire situation is horrible,'' Madeline continued.

''What would you have me do? Scream and shout? Yell at the stationmaster who's done nothing but be as helpful and kind as possible? Is that what you want?''

Her question was followed by Madeline's soft unhappy sigh.

''I feel so incredibly guilty,'' her daughter confessed after a moment.

''Why in heaven's name should you feel anything of the sort?'' It was ludicrous that Madeline was blaming herself for these unfortunate circumstances.

''But, Mother, you're with strangers, instead of family, and I'd hoped—''

''Now stop,'' Cathy said in her sternest voice. ''None of this is your fault. In any case, I'm here in

Abbott and perfectly content. I brought my knitting with me and there are plenty of others for company.''

''But it's Christmas Eve,'' Madeline protested.

Cathy closed her eyes and inhaled sharply. ''Do you honestly believe any Christmas will ever be the same for me without your father?''

''Oh, Mom.'' Her daughter's voice fell. ''Don't mention Daddy, please. It's so hard without him.''

''But life goes on,'' Cathy said, doing her best to sound brave and optimistic.

''I'd wanted to make everything better for you.''

''You have,'' Cathy told her gently. ''I couldn't have stayed at the house alone. I'd rather be in this depot with strangers than spending Christmas with memories I'm not ready to face. And sometime tonight or tomorrow, I'll be with all of you. Now let's stop before we both embarrass ourselves.''

''You'll phone as soon as the tracks are repaired?''

''The minute I hear, you'll be the first to know.''

''Brian and I and the girls will come down to the depot for you.''

''Fine, sweetheart. Now don't you worry, okay?''

Madeline hesitated, then whispered, ''I love you, Mom.''

''I love you, too. Now promise me you won't fret.''

''I'll try.''

''Good.'' After a few words of farewell, Cathy replaced the receiver and returned to her seat. The depot was warm, thanks to the small stove. Those who'd stayed had taken up residence on the hardwood benches. As Cathy reached for her knitting, she battled back a fresh wave of depression.

Madeline was right. It was a dreadful situation, being stuck in a train depot this day of all the days in the year. She glanced around at the others. They appeared just as miserable as she.

Could this really be Christmas?

Four

"The Most Wonderful Day of the Year"

"Hi." A little girl with pigtails and a charming toothless smile sauntered up to Cathy.

"Hello," Cathy said in a friendly voice. Not including the baby, two children remained in the depot. A girl and a boy. The girl bounced about the room like a red rubber ball, but the boy remained glued to his parents' sides.

"What are you doing?" the child asked, slipping onto the wooden bench next to her.

"Knitting. This is a sweater for my granddaughter. She's about your age."

"I'm five."

"So is Lindsay."

"I can read. The kindergarten teacher told Mommy I'm advanced for my age."

"That's wonderful. I'll bet your mother and father are very proud of you." Cathy smiled at the youngster while her fingers continued to work the colorful yarn.

The little girl's head drooped slightly. "My mommy and daddy are divorced now."

Cathy felt the child's confusion and pain. "That's too bad."

She nodded, looking wise beyond her years. "We're going to spend Christmas with my grandma Gibson in Boston."

"Kate." A frazzled young woman approached the little girl. "I hope you weren't bothering this lady."

"Not at all," Cathy assured her.

"My grandma said Santa was coming tonight and bringing me lots of presents." Kate's sweet face lit up with excitement. "Santa'll still come, won't he, even if the train is late?"

"Of course he will," the child's mother told her in a tone that suggested this wasn't the first time she'd reassured her daughter.

"He'll find us even in the storm?"

"He has Rudolph's nose to guide his sleigh, remember?"

Kate nodded.

Cathy let her knitting rest in her lap.

"Can I read to you?" the youngster asked, her eyes huge. "Please?"

"Why, I can't think of anything I'd enjoy more." Cathy could, but it was clear the restless child needed something to take her mind off the situation, and she was happy to listen. Having grandchildren, she could well appreciate the difficulty of keeping a five-year-old entertained in conditions such as these.

Kate raced for her backpack and returned a moment later with her precious book.

"Thank you," Kate's mother whispered. "I'm Elise Jones."

"Hello, Elise. Cathy Norris."

Kate scooted onto the bench between Cathy and her mother and eagerly opened the book. She placed her finger on the first word and started reading aloud with a fluency that suggested this was a much-read and much-loved story.

Cathy smiled down on the little girl. Soon all this frustration and delay would be over. Mr. Kemper would come out from behind his desk and announce that the tracks had been repaired and they'd be on their way. In a few hours she'd be with Madeline and her family, all of this behind her. Somehow, listening to Kate read soothed her, made her feel that today's problems were tolerable. Inconvenient but definitely tolerable.

Kate's voice slowly faded and her eyes closed. She slumped over, her head against Cathy's side. Seconds later the book slipped from her lap and onto the floor.

"Oh, thank heaven, she's going to take a nap, after all," Elise whispered, getting carefully to her feet. She lifted Kate's small legs onto the bench and tucked a spare sweater beneath her head.

"Children can be quite a handful," Cathy murmured, remembering the first time she and Ron had watched their two granddaughters for an entire day while Madeline and Brian attended an investment workshop. The kids had been picked up by four that afternoon, but she and Ron went to bed before eight o'clock, exhausted.

"Being a single mother is no piece of cake," Elise told her. "When Greg and I divorced, I didn't have a clue what would happen. Then he lost his job and had to manage on his unemployment check. He just started working again—but he's so far behind on everything. Now he's having trouble making the child-support payments on time, which only complicates things." Embarrassed she looked away as if she regretted what she'd said. "We wouldn't have Christmas if it wasn't for my mother. I certainly can't afford gifts this year."

The pain that flashed in the younger woman's eyes couldn't be hidden. Cathy realized that, in many ways, Elise's divorce had been as devastating as a death. Feeling a kinship with her, she reached over and squeezed her hand.

Elise recovered quickly, then said with forced enthusiasm, "I've always wanted to know how to knit."

"Would you like me to teach you?" Cathy asked, seizing upon the idea. She'd successfully taught her own three daughters and carried an extra set of needles in her knitting bag. Now was ideal, seeing as they had nothing but time on their hands and Kate was sleeping.

"Now?" Elise asked, flustered. "I mean, I'd love to, but are you sure it isn't too much trouble?"

"Of course not. I've found knitting calms my nerves, especially these past few months since my husband died."

"I'm sorry about your husband," Elise said, real sympathy in her voice.

"Yes, I am, too. I miss him dreadfully." With a sense of purpose Cathy reached for her spare needles. "Would you like to start now?"

Elise nodded. "Why not?"

Cathy pulled out a ball of yarn. "Then let me show you how to cast on stitches. It isn't the least bit difficult."

Len had trouble not watching the clock. They'd been in Abbott a total of four hours, with no further word regarding their situation. The stationmaster, Clayton Kemper, had turned out to be a kindhearted soul. He'd made a fresh pot of coffee and offered it to anyone who wanted a cup, free of charge.

Len had declined. Stressed as he was, the last thing he needed was caffeine. Plenty of others took advantage of Kemper's generosity, though. They were a motley group, Len noted. The widow, dressed in her gray wool coat with her knitting and her sad but friendly smile. The divorced mother and her little girl.

The grumpy sales rep. The young couple with the baby, the hippie and his wife, the elderly black couple plus an assortment of others.

Kemper walked by with the coffeepot on a tray. "You sure I can't interest you in a cup, young man?"

"I'm sure."

"I found a deck of cards. How about that?"

Len nodded eagerly. "That'd be great." Cards would be a welcome way to pass the time. He sometimes played solitaire and enjoyed two or three different versions of the game. At the mention of cards, the sales rep, who sat close by, looked up from his laptop. Maybe Len could talk two or three of the others into a game of pinochle or poker.

"You play pinochle?" he asked Matt.

"And canasta, hearts, bridge—whatever you want."

"I wouldn't mind playing," Nick volunteered.

"Come to think of it, I've got an old card table in the back room," Kemper said when he returned with the cards. "And a couple of chairs, too, if you need 'em. I should have thought of this earlier. You folks must be bored out of your minds."

A fourth man joined them, and with a little rearranging they soon had the table set up. That was followed by the sound of cards being shuffled and the occasional scrape of a chair as they settled down to a friendly game of pinochle.

* * *

Kelly Berry's arms ached from holding the baby. The carrier seat was still on the train, but she hadn't asked Nick to bring it in. He'd already gone outside once and seemed reluctant to venture into the storm again. Besides, he was busy playing cards.

Kelly wondered, not for the first time, if they'd *ever* adjust to parenthood. The whole experience was so…different from what she'd expected. Desperately longing for a child of their own, they'd dreamed and hungered to the point that Kelly felt their marriage would be incomplete without a family. Now, after three months with a fussy, colicky infant, she was ready to admit her spirits were the lowest they'd been in years.

She'd always believed a baby would bring her and Nick closer together. The baby would be a living symbol of their love and commitment to each other, the culmination of their marriage. Instead, Brittany seemed to have driven a wedge between them. Not long ago their world had revolved entirely around each other; these days, it revolved around Brittany. Caring for the baby demanded all their energy, all their time.

Her arms tightened around her daughter, and a surge of love filled her heart. She and Nick felt overwhelmed because this was so new, Kelly told herself. In a few months everything would be easier—for both of them. While confident of Nick's love, Kelly knew he found it difficult to deal with the changes that had come into their marriage since the adoption.

"Would you like me to hold the baby for a while?" The older woman sat down next to her. "I'm Cathy Norris. You must be exhausted."

"Kelly Berry." She hesitated. "You wouldn't mind?"

"Not at all," Cathy said, taking the sleeping infant from her arms. She gazed down at Brittany and smiled. "She's certainly beautiful, and her little red outfit is delightful."

"Thank you," Kelly said, truly grateful. She'd enjoyed dressing Brittany for the holiday season. She could've spent a fortune if Nick had let her, but her ever-practical husband had been the voice of reason. Not that *he* wasn't guilty of spoiling their daughter.

"She certainly resembles your husband."

Kelly glowed with happiness. "I think so, too."

With an ease that Kelly envied, Cathy Norris held Brittany against her shoulder, gently rubbing her back. Brittany shifted her head to one side and her tiny mouth made small sucking sounds. Once more Kelly's heart stirred with love.

She felt someone's gaze and glanced up to find Nick watching her. When he realized he had her attention, he smiled. His eyes softened as he looked at their daughter.

They *would* be all right, Kelly thought. This was their dream; it was just that after waiting and planning all these years, they hadn't been quite as ready for the reality as they'd assumed.

Clayton Kemper walked out of the station and returned almost immediately, a shovel in his hand. "Good news!" he shouted.

Every head in the room shot up, every face alight with expectation, Kelly's included. Some people were already on their feet, reaching for bags of colorfully wrapped gifts.

"The storm's died down. It's stopped snowing."

"Does that mean we can get out of here any sooner?" Matt McHugh demanded.

"Well, it's bound to help the repair crew."

The happy anticipation sank to the pit of Kelly's stomach. *Oh, please,* she prayed, *don't let us end up spending our first Christmas with Brittany stuck in a train depot. Don't let this be our Christmas.*

Five

"O Christmas Tree"

The news that the snow had stopped falling should have cheered Len Dawber, but it didn't. Instead, his mood took an immediate dive. He'd figured that with the storm passing, the train would leave soon. It didn't appear to be the case.

His interest in the card game died and he got up to give his seat to someone else, but no one seemed keen to play anymore. Before long, Nick Berry had the deck of cards and sat alone, flipping through them in a listless game of solitaire.

His frustration mounting, Len approached the counter. Clayton Kemper glanced up. "Can I get you anything?"

"How about some information?" Matt McHugh asked, moving to Len's side. "We've been here six hours. There must be *something* you can tell us by now." He clenched his fist and rested it on the counter. "You've got to realize how impossible this situation is for us."

Kemper shrugged helplessly. "I don't know what to tell you."

"Isn't there someone you could phone?" The plaintive voice of a woman came from behind them. Len looked over his shoulder and recognized the mother of the little boy, who still clung to her side.

"Find out what you can," Matt insisted. "You owe us that much."

"Surely there's someone you can call," the elderly black man said.

Tension filled the room as more people stood up and started walking about. The baby Cathy Norris held awoke suddenly and shattered the air with a piercing cry. Cathy tried to quiet the infant, but it did no good. The young mother couldn't do any better. The baby's cries clawed at already taut nerves.

"Kindly keep that baby quiet, would you?" Len wasn't sure who'd said that; painful as the baby's shrieking was, he felt a fleeting sympathy for the mother.

"Do something," Nick snapped at his wife.

"I'm trying," Kelly said, glaring back at him with a hurt look.

"I've got to get out of here," Nick said, and stalked outside, letting the door slam in his wake.

"We need information," Len pressed Kemper again.

"At least give us an idea how much longer it could

be,'' Matt added. "In case you've forgotten, it's Christmas Eve.''

Kemper was clearly at a loss and for an instant Len felt sympathy for him, too, but he felt even worse for himself. He'd been looking forward to this night for weeks. He wanted it to be the most beautiful and romantic evening of his life. Instead, he'd probably be spending it in this train station somewhere in New Hampshire.

Kemper raised his hands to quiet the murmurs of discontent. "I'll make a few phone calls and see what I can find out.''

"You should have done that long before now,'' Matt said irritably.

Len was in full agreement. This damned waiting had gone on long enough. The minute he had a definite answer, he'd call Amy again. Even if he *didn't* have an answer, he was phoning Amy. He needed to hear the sound of her voice, needed to know this nightmare would soon be over and they'd be together—if not for Christmas, then soon.

Len returned to his seat and Matt followed him. "This isn't exactly my idea of Christmas Eve,'' the older man muttered, more to himself than his companion.

"I don't think any of us could have anticipated this.''

It didn't take Kemper long to connect with someone, Len noticed. The stationmaster was on the phone five minutes. He nodded once in a while, then scowled and wrote something down on a piece of paper. When he'd finished, he walked toward the pot-bellied stove.

Every eye in the room followed him. "Well," he said, with a deep expressive sigh, "there really isn't any news I can give you."

"No news is good news?" Cathy suggested hopefully.

"No news is no news," Matt McHugh returned tartly.

"You were talking to someone," Len said. "They must've had something to say...."

"Only what I found out earlier, that the break in the line is more serious than was originally determined."

"Isn't there anything you can suggest? How long should we expect to wait? Give us your best estimate. Surely you've seen breakdowns like this before." Len's voice thinned with frustration. He noticed a number of people nodding as he spoke.

"Well," Kemper said thoughtfully, "you're right, I have seen plenty of breakdowns over the years. Each one's different. But we've got a full crew working on this one, despite the fact that it's Christmas Eve."

"That's encouraging, anyway," Elise Jones said. "It isn't like any of us planned to spend the holidays here, you know."

"I know, I know." Kemper looked out over the

group and seemed to recognize that he wouldn't be off the hook until he gave these people some kind of answer. "My best guess is sometime after midnight."

"Midnight!" Matt shouted.

He wasn't the only one who reacted with anger. But Len barely reacted at all; he felt as though the wind had been knocked clear out of him. Slowly he sank onto the bench and closed his eyes. He no longer knew if the airline could even get him a seat. Because of the snowstorm he'd missed his original flight. Because of the train's delay, he hadn't made the standby flight, either. Nor could he book another. Not until he could give the airline a time.

This felt like the worst day of his life.

Nick knew he was a fool, snapping at his wife in front of a room full of strangers and then stalking out of the train depot like a two-year-old having a tantrum. He'd caught the shocked look in Kelly's eyes. It was uncharacteristic behavior for him, but he'd just been feeling so...on edge. Then he'd lost control because someone had shouted at Kelly to keep Brittany quiet.

What upset him was that he'd been thinking the same thing himself. He wanted her to do something, anything, to stop Brittany's crying. The baby had been contentedly asleep for a few hours, and he supposed he'd been lulled into a false sense of peace. Then she'd awakened, and it seemed that every ounce of composure he'd managed to scrape together had vanished.

He'd say one thing for his daughter. She had an incredible sense of timing. Why she'd pick that precise moment to start wailing, he'd never know. She was a fragile little thing, but obviously had the lungs of a tuba player.

It had felt as though everyone in the room was glaring at him and Kelly with malice, although in retrospect, he thought his own frustrations had probably made him misread their reactions. Everything in life had come hard for Nick; why should fatherhood be any different? He'd been raised in a series of foster homes and the only reason he'd been able to go on with his schooling was because of a scholarship. He'd graduated while holding down two part-time jobs and now worked as a scientist for a pharmaceutical company. He'd met Kelly when they were both in college. He still considered it a miracle that this beautiful woman loved him. For years now, her love had been the constant in his life, his emotional anchor, his sanctuary.

The intense cold had soaked through his coat. He kicked at the snow, depressed and angry with himself. Kelly deserved a better husband, and Brittany sure as hell needed a more loving father.

He was about to go back inside the station when the door opened and Clayton Kemper walked out.

"You're leaving?" Nick asked, shocked that the stationmaster would desert them at a time like this.

Clayton Kemper looked more than a little guilty. "My shift was over an hour ago and the missus is wanting me home."

Talk about deserting the ship. "Someone else is coming, right?"

"Oh, sure. Don't you worry. Someone'll be by to check up on you folks, but it might not be for a while." Having said that, he headed down the steps, then glanced back over his shoulder and called, "Merry Christmas."

Nick stared at the man in disbelief. This had to be the worst Christmas of his entire life! Trapped with a cranky newborn and a wife who refused to see reason. If it'd been up to him, the three of them would at least have been in a motel room, comfortable and warm. But Kelly hadn't wanted to leave the station, certain the repairs wouldn't take long. Now it was too late. The guy with the long hair and his wife had already made inquiries. Apparently every hotel for miles around was full.

This optimistic bent of Kelly's had always been a problem. He'd been ready to give up on the fertility clinic long before she agreed. The expense had been horrific, and he didn't mean just the financial aspects. Emotionally Kelly was a wreck two weeks out of every month. Only when he was able to talk her into accepting their situation and applying to an adoption agency had she gotten off the emotional roller coaster.

Nick had almost given up hope himself—and then they received the phone call about Brittany. That five-minute conversation had changed their lives forever.

He found himself grinning at the memory. Kelly was the one who'd been cool and calm while he'd sat there trembling. He'd never experienced any excitement even close to what he'd felt when he learned they finally had a baby.

The first instant he saw Brittany, he'd been swept by a love so powerful it was beyond comprehension. Yet here he was, three months later, acting like a dolt and snapping at his wife in public.

That wasn't his only offense, either. For most of the afternoon, he'd ignored Kelly and the baby, wanting to escape them both. He wasn't proud of himself; he'd ignored their needs, leaving Kelly to care for their daughter on her own while he brooded and behaved like a spoiled child.

With that in mind, he boarded the train, walked down the narrow aisle and got the baby seat down from the storage compartment. Kelly's arms must be tired from holding Brittany. He wished he'd thought of this sooner.

Hauling in a deep breath, he walked back into the station and stomped the snow from his boots. When he looked up, he discovered Kelly staring at him, her lips tight, but her eyes forgiving.

"I'm sorry," he whispered as he sat beside her. He gazed down at Brittany, who gazed back at him, her blue eyes wide and curious. His daughter seemed to recognize him, and she, at least, didn't know enough to realize what a cantankerous fool he'd been the past few hours. He offered her his finger, which she gripped eagerly with her little hand.

"I'm sorry, too," Kelly whispered back, sounding close to tears.

Nick set the baby seat on the floor and placed his arm around his wife's shoulders. She leaned her head against him. "I don't know what came over me," he murmured, "I wish we were anyplace but here."

"Me, too," Kelly said.

"Amy?"

Len felt a surge of relief and unmistakable joy at the sound of her "hello."

"Are you in Boston?" she asked excitedly. "When can you catch a flight home?"

"I'm still in Abbott," Len said, his happiness evaporating quickly with the reality of this long day. He was trapped, a hostage to circumstances beyond his control.

"You're still in Abbott?" Amy sounded ready to weep. "Oh, Len, will you ever get home for Christmas?"

"I don't know," he told her, trying to keep his own

hopes alive—and failing. It seemed everything was against him.

"Yes," he said suddenly, emphatically. For a moment he didn't know where this optimism had come from. Then he did. It was his overwhelming need to be with Amy. "I *will* get home for Christmas." He wasn't about to let the storm, the damaged tracks or anything else ruin his leave. "I'll be home for Christmas, Amy. You can count on it."

He could almost feel her spirits rise. "Your girl in Rawhide will be waiting for you, sailor man."

"You're more than my girl in Rawhide," Len said. "You're my one and only girl. Period!"

She said nothing after his declaration. "Do you mean that, Len?" she finally asked.

"With all my heart." He was tempted to tell her about the diamond, but that would ruin his surprise, and he didn't want to propose over the phone. It just didn't seem near good enough. He wanted her to see the love in his eyes and watch her face when she saw the ring.

"Oh, Len," she whispered.

"Listen, would you call my mom and dad and tell them I still don't know when I'll be home?"

"Sure. Listen, since you can't be here, I'll go back to the nursing home tonight and play the piano for everyone. They wanted to sing Christmas carols but couldn't find any staff willing to take time away from their families."

Len loved her all the more for her generous heart.

"I can't see sitting around home and moping," she explained.

"Sing a Christmas carol for me."

"I will," she said, and her voice softened.

There was a beep in his ear and Len knew he had only a couple of minutes left on his calling card.

"Oh, Len," Amy said. "Time's running out."

"Remember, I'll see you as soon as I can," he said, ready to hang up.

"Len, Len..."

"Yes? What is it?"

"Len," she said, her voice catching, "I...love you. I was going to wait until tonight to tell you, but I want you to know right now. You might be in New Hampshire and me here in Rawhide, but that doesn't matter, because you have my heart with you wherever you are."

The line went dead. Len wasn't sure if she'd hung up or if the time had simply expired.

"I love you, too, Amy," he said into the silent phone, knowing she couldn't hear the words. Somehow he was certain she could feel his heart responding to hers. Soon she'd know how very much he loved his Amy Sue.

Len replaced the receiver and turned around to face the room. Everyone seemed in a dour mood.

The door burst open just then and a smiling, light-hearted Clayton Kemper walked in. He glanced around and beamed proudly at the group of weary travelers.

"I was on my way home when I ran across this," he said cheerfully. He stuck his hand out the door and dragged in the sorriest-looking Christmas tree Len had ever seen.

One side of the evergreen was bare, the top had split and two branches spiked in opposite directions, resembling bug antennae.

"The man in the Christmas-tree lot gave it to me for a buck."

"You got overcharged," Matt McHugh muttered. His words were followed by a few short laughs and a general feeling of agreement.

"That may well be," Kemper said, not letting their lack of enthusiasm dampen his spirit. "But it seemed to me that since you folks are stuck here on Christmas Eve, you might as well make the best of it."

"That tree looks like it's in the same shape we're in," Elise Jones said dryly.

"The tree is yours to do with as you wish," Kemper told them. "Merry Christmas to you all."

No one thought to thank him, Len noticed.

The sad little tree stood in the center of the room, bare and forlorn, wounded and ugly. He'd have to go along with Elise. The Christmas tree did resemble them—and their attitude.

Five-year-old Kate Jones walked over to it and stood with her arms akimbo, staring at the limp branches. Then, apparently having come to some sort of decision, she turned to confront the disgruntled group.

"I think it's a beautiful tree," she announced. "It just needs a little help." She removed the red bow from the top of her head and pinned it to the nearest branch.

Despite himself, Len grinned. On closer examination, the kid was right. The tree wasn't nearly as ugly as he'd first thought.

Six

"Sing We Now of Christmas"

Most everyone ignored the Christmas tree, Cathy Norris mused sadly. Except for Kate... Then Kelly walked over and silently added a rattle. She took her time finding just the right spot for it, choosing to hang it directly in the middle, opposite Kate's hair bow.

Turning to the others, she smiled and said, "Come on, you guys, it's Christmas Eve."

"She's right," Nick said, and joined his wife. He bounced the baby gently in his arms, and Brittany grinned and reached for his bright green muffler. Nick removed it, handed the baby to Kelly and placed the muffler on the tree, stretching it out as if it were the finest decorative strand. He wove it between the lower branches of the fir, the wool fringe dangling like green wool tinsel.

Len surveyed the tree, then stepped up and added his white cap, settling it near the top, where it sat jauntily.

The elderly black man moved forward next and added his tie clasp. He clipped it to the branch in an upright position like a clothespin, stepped back and nodded once, apparently pleased with the effect. "Hey, this tree doesn't look so bad."

Soon others became creative about decorating the Christmas tree. Cathy cut strips of red yarn and with Kate's help draped the strands over as many branches as they could reach.

Even the grumpy salesman pitched in. Cathy saw him with the small pair of scissors on his Swiss Army knife, folding and cutting memos into paper snow-flakes, then hanging them on the tree with dental floss. Actually they looked quite attractive against the backdrop of red yarn.

It wasn't long before every branch sprouted some sort of odd decoration. True, it wasn't a traditional Christmas tree, but it seemed to possess amazing powers. The scowls and complaints of moments ear-lier were now replaced by smiles and animated chat-ter.

"I think my daughter's right," Elise said, walking over to more closely examine their handiwork. "This is actually a beautiful tree."

The little boy, around three or four, who'd stayed close by his parents the entire day, clapped in delight.

Cathy noticed several smiles.

"I'm hungry," Kate whispered to her mother.

Worrying about their situation as she had for most

of the day, Cathy hadn't given any thought to food until the youngster mentioned it. She apparently wasn't the only one.

"What about dinner?" Cathy asked, glancing about the room. It looked as though they'd been left to fend for themselves. Mr. Kemper had said someone would come by to check on them, but so far no one had.

"Nothing's going to be open tonight," Matt McHugh grumbled. "Not on Christmas Eve."

"Especially not with the storm and all earlier," Len put in.

Cathy could feel the mood of the room, so recently elevated, plunge. Already those who'd moved closer to the Christmas tree were sliding away to slump on benches by the walls.

"Now, that does bring up an interesting prospect," Cathy said, speaking to the entire group for the first time. "I'm Cathy Norris, by the way. I'm going to visit my daughter and her family in Boston, and I just happened to bring along four dozen of her favorite shortbread cookies. Somehow, I don't think she'd mind my sharing them with all of you."

She brought out the tin and pried open the lid.

"My wife and I have several oranges," the elderly black man said. "We can share those. Since we're going to be eating together, it's only appropriate that we introduce ourselves. My name's Sam Givens and my wife's Louise."

"Thank you, Sam and Louise," Cathy said. "Anyone else?"

"I'm Matt McHugh. I was given a fruitcake on my last sales call," Matt surprised her by saying. "I would've thrown the damn thing out, but one of my kids likes the stuff. I can cut that up if anyone's interested."

"Well, I'm quite fond of fruitcake," Kelly Berry said.

Although the depot office was locked, the counter was free and Cathy placed the tin of cookies there. Matt took out the fruitcake and sliced it with his Swiss Army knife. Sam Givens brought over the oranges, then peeled and sectioned them.

Elise Jones collected paper towels from the rest room to use as napkins. Soon more and more food appeared. It seemed almost everyone had something to share. A plate of beautifully decorated chocolates. A white cardboard box filled with pink divinity and homemade fudge. Then a tin of peanuts and a bag of pretzels. Len added a package of cinnamon-flavored gum.

A crooked line formed and they all helped themselves, taking bits and pieces of each dish. It wasn't much, but it helped do more than dull the edge of their hunger. It proved, to Cathy at least, that there was hope for them. That banding together they could get through this and even have a good time.

"My mother's serving prime rib right about now,"

Elise lamented as she took an orange segment and a handful of peanuts.

"And to think she's missing out on Matt Mc-Hugh's fruitcake," Cathy said, and was delighted by the responding laugh that echoed down the line. Even Matt chuckled. An hour ago Cathy would have thought that impossible.

"I never thought I'd say this about fruitcake," the young sailor said, saluting Matt with a slice, "but this ain't half-bad."

"What about my peanuts?" the guy with long hair asked. "I spent hours slaving over a hot stove to make those."

Everyone smiled and the silly jokes continued.

"Quiet," Nick said suddenly, jumping to his feet. "I hear something."

"A train?" Matt teased.

"'Do you hear what I hear?'" Someone sang.

"I'm serious."

It didn't take Cathy long to pick up the faint sound of voices singing. "Someone's coming," she announced.

"Carolers?" Kelly asked. "On a night like this? For us?"

"No night more perfect," Cathy murmured. Years ago she and Ron had been members of the church choir. Each holiday season the choir had toured nursing homes and hospitals, giving short performances. They'd been active in their church for a number of years. Unfortunately their attendance had slipped after Ron retired, then stopped completely when he became seriously ill. And afterward...well, afterward Cathy simply didn't have the heart for it.

For the first time since the funeral, she felt the need to return. This insight was like an unexpected gift, and it had come to her at the sound of the carolers' voices.

The door opened and a group of fifteen or so entered the train depot.

"Hello, everyone." A man with a bushy gray mustache and untamed gray hair stepped forward. "I'm Dean Owen. Clayton Kemper's a friend of mine and he mentioned you folks were stranded. This is the teen choir from the Regular Baptist Church. Since we weren't able to get out last night because of the snow, we thought we'd make a few rounds this evening. How's everyone doing?"

"Great."

"As good as can be expected."

"Hangin' in there."

"I love your Christmas tree," one of the girls said. She was about sixteen, with long blond hair in a ponytail and twinkling eyes.

"We decorated it ourselves," Kate said, pointing to her hair bow. "That's mine."

"Would anyone mind if I took a picture?" the girl asked, pulling a disposable camera from her coat pocket.

"This is something that's got to be seen to be believed," Matt whispered to Cathy. "Actually I wouldn't mind having a copy of it myself."

"Me, too."

"Shall we make it a family photo?" Elise asked.

A chorus of yes's and no's followed, but within a minute the ragtag group had gathered around the tree. Cathy ran a comb through her hair and added a dash of lipstick. Others, too, reviewed their appearance as they assembled for the photograph, jostling each other good-naturedly.

What amazed Cathy were the antics that went on before the picture was taken. They behaved like a group of teenagers themselves. Len held up the V for peace sign behind Nick's head. Even Matt managed a crooked smile. For that matter, so did Cathy. Someone joked and she laughed. That made her realize how long it'd been since she'd allowed herself to be happy. *Too long. Ron wouldn't want that.*

The girl took four snapshots. Before long the development of the film had been paid for and she had a list of names and addresses to send copies of the photo. Cathy's name was there along with everyone else's. She wanted something tangible to remember this eventful day—the oddest Christmas Eve she'd spent in her entire life.

"We thought we'd deliver a bit of cheer," Dean said, once the photo arrangements were finished.

Their coming had done exactly that. The travelers

gathered around without anyone's direction, positioning the benches in a way that allowed them all to see the singers.

The choir assembled in three rows of five each and began with "Silent Night," sung in three-part harmony. Cathy had heard the old carol all her life, but never had it sounded more beautiful than it did this evening. Without accompaniment, without embellishment, simple, plain—and incredibly lovely. With the beautiful words came a sense of camaraderie and joy, a sense that this night was truly special.

This *was* a holy night.

"Silent Night" was followed by "The Little Drummer Boy," then "Joy to the World," one carol flowing smoothly into another, ending with "We Wish You a Merry Christmas."

While Cathy and the others applauded loudly, Kate in a burst of childish enthusiasm spontaneously rushed forward and hugged Dean's knees. "That was so pretty," she squealed, her delight contagious.

Len jumped to his feet, continuing the applause. Soon the others stood, too, including Cathy.

The small choir seemed overwhelmed by their appreciation.

"This is the first time we ever got a standing ovation," the girl with the camera said, smiling at her friends. "I didn't realize we were that good."

"Sing more," Kate pleaded. "Do you know 'Rudolph the Red-Nosed Reindeer'?"

"Can you sing it with us?" Dean bent down and asked Kate.

The child nodded enthusiastically, and Dean had her stand in front of the choir. "Sing away."

"Join in, everyone," he suggested next, turning to face his small audience.

Cathy and the others didn't need any encouragement. Their voices blended with those of the choir as if they'd sung together for weeks. "Rudolph" led to other Christmas songs—"Silver Bells," "Deck the Halls," and the time passed quickly.

When they finished, the choir members brought out paper cups and thermoses of hot chocolate. No sooner had the hot drink been poured than the station door opened again.

"So Clayton was right." A petite older woman, with a cap of white hair and eyelids painted the brightest shade of blue Cathy had ever seen, entered the room. Two other women filed in after her.

"I'm Greta Barnes," the leader said, "and we're from the Veterans of Foreign Wars Women's Auxiliary."

"We've brought you folks dinner," another woman told them.

"Now you're talking!" Len Dawber shouted. "Sorry, folks, but a slice of fruitcake and a few pretzels didn't quite fill me up."

"Made for a great appetizer, though," Nick said.

"The food's out in the car. Would someone help

carry it in?'' Greta asked. She didn't have to ask for volunteers a second time. Nick, Matt and Len were up before any of the other men had a chance. A couple of minutes later they were back inside, their arms loaded with boxes.

''It's not much,'' one of the other women said apologetically as she set a huge pot of soup on the counter. ''We didn't get much notice.''

''We're grateful for whatever you brought us,'' Sam assured the women. Louise nodded in agreement.

''Luckily the family had plenty of clam chowder left over,'' the older of Greta's friends said. ''The soup's a Christmas Eve tradition in our house, and I can't help it, I always cook up more than enough.''

''Eleanor's soup is the best in the state,'' Greta declared.

''There's sandwiches, too,'' the third woman said, unpacking one of the smaller boxes.

''And seeing that no one knows when the repairs on those tracks are going to be finished,'' the spry older woman added, ''we decided to bring along some blankets and pillows.''

''All the comforts of home,'' Matt muttered, but the caustic edge that had laced his comments earlier in the day had vanished.

''I must say you folks are certainly good sports about all this.''

Considering that this change in attitude had only

recently come about, none of them leaped to their feet to accept credit.

"Like I said earlier," Matt told her, speaking for the group, "we're making the best of it."

"We're very grateful for the pillows and blankets," Cathy put in.

"The food, too," several others said.

The church choir stayed and helped pass around the sandwiches, which were delicious. Cathy ate half a tuna-salad sandwich, then half a turkey one. She was amazed at how big her appetite was. Food, like almost everything since Ron's death, had become a necessity and not an enjoyment.

When the teen choir left, it was with a cheery wave and the promise that everyone who'd asked for a picture would be sure to receive one. With a responsible kindhearted man like Dean Owen as their leader, Cathy was confident it would come about.

The soup and sandwiches disappeared quickly. Three other men helped pack up the leftovers and carted the boxes out to the car.

"You sure we can't get you anything else?" Greta asked before she headed outside.

"You've done more than enough."

"Thank Mr. Kemper for us," Len said, ready to escort the older women to their vehicle.

With many shouts of "Merry Christmas," everyone waved the Auxiliary ladies goodbye.

Len returned, leaning against the door when it

closed. Cathy watched as he paused and glanced about the room. "You know," he said, not speaking to anyone in particular, "I almost feel sorry for all those people who decided to stay in hotels. They've missed out on the best Christmas Eve I can ever remember."

Seven

"Santa Claus Is Coming to Town"

The station seemed unnaturally quiet after the choir and the members of the VFW Women's Auxiliary had left. The lively chatter and shared laughter that had filled the room died down to a low hum.

Matt knew he should phone home, that he'd delayed it as long as he dared. With the time difference between the east and west coasts, it wasn't quite four in the afternoon in Los Angeles. The dread that settled over him depleted the sense of well-being he'd experienced over the past few hours.

He didn't look forward to a telephone confrontation with Pam, but as far as he could see there was no avoiding one. He could almost hear her voice, starting low and quickly gaining volume until it reached a shrill, near-hysterical pitch.

He wished things could be different, but he knew she'd start in on him, and then, despite his best efforts, he'd retaliate. Soon their exchange would escalate into a full-blown fight.

His feet felt weighted as he crossed the station to the row of pay phones. He slipped his credit card through the appropriate slot, punched in his home number and waited for the line to connect.

The phone rang twice, three times, then four before the answering machine came on. Bored, he tapped his foot while he listened to the message he'd recorded earlier in the year. When he heard the signal, he was ready. "Pam, it's Matt. I'm sorry about this, but I got caught in the snowstorm that struck Maine yesterday. The flights out of Bangor were canceled, so the airline put me on a train for Boston. Now the train tracks are out and I don't have a clue when I'll be home. As soon as I reach Boston, probably sometime Christmas morning, I'll phone and let you know when to expect me. I'm sorry about this, but it's out of my control. Kiss the kids for me and I'll see you as soon as I can."

The relief that came over him at not getting caught in a verbal battle with his wife was like an unexpected gift. This wasn't how it should be, but he felt powerless to change the dynamics of their marriage. Somewhere along the road the partnership they'd once shared had fallen apart. He wasn't the only one who felt miserable; he knew that. The look in Pam's eyes as he'd walked through the house, suitcase in hand, had told him he wasn't the only one thinking about a separation.

His mood was oppressive by the time he returned to his seat.

"What about Santa?" Matt heard Kate ask her mother.

"Honey, he's still coming to Grandma's house." Kate's mother was busy making up a bed for her daughter. She placed a pillow at one end of the bench and arranged the blanket so the little girl could sleep between its folds.

"But, Mom, I'm *not* at Grandma Gibson's house— I'm *here*. Santa might not know."

Elise apparently needed a minute to think about that. "Grandma will have to tell him."

"But what if Santa decides to try to find me here, instead of leaving my presents with Grandma?"

"Kate, please, can't you just trust that you're going to get your gifts?"

Arms crossed, the child shook her head stubbornly. "No, I can't," she said, her voice as serious as the expression on her face. "You told me Daddy was going to come see me before we left and he didn't."

"Honey, I don't have any control over what your father says and does. I'm sorry he disappointed you."

Her look said it wasn't the first time mother and child had been let down.

Kate started to whimper.

"Sweetheart, please," Elise whispered. She seemed close to breaking down herself. She picked up her daughter and held her close. As she gently rocked the little girl, her eyes shone with unshed tears. "Santa won't forget you."

"Daddy did."

"No, honey, I'm sure he didn't, not really."

"Then why didn't he come like he said?"

"Because…" Elise began, then hesitated and forcefully expelled her breath. "It's complicated."

"Everything's complicated since you and Daddy divorced."

Matt felt like an eavesdropper, yet he couldn't tune out the conversation between mother and child. Part of him yearned to let Kate use his credit card to phone her father, but if he suggested that, Elise would know he'd been listening in.

Hearing Kate cry about being forgotten by her dad left Matt to wonder if this would be his own children's future should he and Pam decide to split up. He didn't want a divorce, never had. But it was obvious they couldn't continue the way they'd been going—belittling each other, arguing, eroding the foundation of their love and commitment.

"Why didn't Daddy come see me like he said he would?" Kate persisted.

Elise took her time answering. "Your daddy was embarrassed."

"Embarrassed?"

"He felt bad."

"About what?"

"Being late helping to pay the bills. He didn't

come see you because...well, because I don't think he could afford to buy you anything for Christmas, and he didn't want you to be disappointed in him because he didn't have a gift.''

Kate mulled that over for a while, nibbling her bottom lip. ''I love him and I didn't have a gift for him, either.''

''Your daddy loves you, Kate, that much I know.''

''Can I talk to him myself?''

Elise took a deep breath. ''You can phone him when we reach Grandma's house, and you can tell him about spending the night in the train depot. He'll want to hear about all your adventures on Christmas Eve.''

Matt considered what would happen to his relationship with his children if he and Pam went their separate ways. The love he felt for Rachel and Jimmy ran deep, and the idea of Pam having to make excuses for him...

His thoughts tumbled to an abrupt halt. That was exactly what Pam had been forced to do the afternoon he'd left for Maine. Jimmy had been counting on him to attend the school Christmas program and, instead, he'd raced off to the airport. Matt's stomach knotted, and he sat back, wiping a hand down his face.

A whispered discussion broke out between the widow and the elderly couple who'd supplied the oranges. Matt had no idea what was going on and, caught up in his own musing, didn't much care.

Not long afterward, he discovered that a few of the senior crowd had decided to take this matter of Christmas for the two children into their own hands.

Cathy walked by Kate, paused suddenly and held one hand to her ear. "Did you hear something?" she asked the youngster.

"Not me," Kate answered.

"I think it's bells."

Elise cupped her ear. "Reindeer feet?"

"Bells," Cathy returned pointedly.

"Yes," Louise piped up. "It's definitely the sound of bells. What could it be?"

They weren't going to get any Academy Award nominations, but they did manage to convince the children.

"I hear bells!" the other child called. "I do, I do." It was the first time the little boy had spoken all day.

Kate sat up straight on her mother's lap. "I hear them, too."

Matt had to admit the two old ladies really had him going; he could almost hear them himself. Then he realized he really *could* hear the jingle of bells.

A knock sounded loudly on the station door. "I'll get it." Sam eagerly stepped to the door. He opened it a couple of inches, nodded a few times and looked over his shoulder. "Do we have a little girl named Kate here and a boy...Charlie?"

"Charles," his mother corrected.

"Kate and Charles," Sam informed the mysterious

visitor no one was allowed to see. "As a matter of fact, Kate and Charles *are* here," Sam said loudly. "You do…of course. I'll see to it personally. Now don't you worry, you have plenty of other deliveries to make tonight. You'd best be on your way."

Matt glanced around and noticed that Nick Berry was missing…and he seemed to remember that their baby had a rattle with bells inside.

The room went quiet as Sam closed the door, and the jingling receded. He had a pillowcase in one hand, with a couple of wrapped gifts inside. "That was Santa Claus," he announced. "He heard that Kate and Charles were stuck here on Christmas Eve. Santa wanted them to know he hadn't forgotten them."

"Did he bring my presents?" Kate sprang off her mother's lap and ran toward Sam, still standing near the door.

Charles joined her, gazing up at the man with hopeful eyes.

"Santa wanted me to tell you he left plenty of gifts at your Grandma Gibson's house, Kate, but he didn't want you to worry that he'd missed you, so he dropped this off." He thrust his arm into the pillowcase and produced a wrapped box.

Matt recognized it right away as one he'd seen poking out of Cathy Norris's carry-on bag when she'd removed the tin of cookies.

"I believe this one is for you, Charles," Sam said. The second gift went to the four-year-old. The boy raced back to his parents and dropped to his knees. He tore into the wrapping paper, scattering pieces in all directions. The minute Charles saw the rubber dinosaur, he cried out in delight and hugged it to his chest.

Kate, on the other hand, opened her present with delicate precision, carefully removing the ribbon first and placing it on the tree. Next came the wrapping paper. Matt couldn't figure out how she did it, but she managed to pull off the Christmas wrap without tearing it even once. When she saw the Barbie doll, she looked up at her mother and smiled wonderingly.

"Daddy must have given it to Santa. This is what I told him I wanted."

"I'm sure he did." Elise was gracious enough to concur.

Matt didn't know what had gone wrong in this woman's marriage, but it wasn't difficult to see the pain that divorce had brought into her life. Could bring into his own, if he allowed it to happen.

Cathy and the elderly couple exchanged smiles that their small ploy had worked. Actually Matt was touched by their generosity; they'd obviously given up Christmas presents meant for their own grandchildren.

He wasn't sure what prompted the idea, but he reached for his briefcase. "As a matter of fact, Santa left a few goodies with me, too. Is anyone interested in a sample of the latest software from MicroChip International?''

It didn't take long to discover that a number of people were.

''Are you sure, man?'' the ex-hippie asked. ''This is worth a good two hundred bucks in the store.''

''Five hundred, actually,'' Matt said. ''Consider it compliments of the company.''

''We've got extra pictures of the baby, if anyone would like,'' Nick offered.

''Sure,'' Len said. ''Amy—my fiancée—is crazy about babies.'' He took one and so did Cathy, Elise and several others.

As had happened earlier with the food, a variety of gifts, some wrapped and others not, started to appear. The joking and laughter continued during the impromptu gift exchange. By the end, everyone had both given and received at least one gift.

Sam, who'd stayed in the background most of the day, stepped forward with a worn Bible in his hand. ''This being the night of our Savior's birth,'' he said, ''I thought we might like to listen to the account of the first Christmas.''

Most people nodded in silent agreement. Sam pulled out a chair and set it close to their Christmas tree, then perched a pair of glasses on his nose.

The room hushed as he began to read. His rich resonant voice echoed through the depot. Everyone listened with an attentiveness Matt found amazing.

When he'd finished, Sam reverently closed the Bible and removed his glasses, tucking them into his shirt pocket. "It seems to me that we all have something in common with Mary and Joseph. They, too, were weary travelers and there wasn't any room for them at the inn." He paused and held up one hand. "I checked earlier and every room in this town has been booked for the night."

There were grins and murmurs at his remark. Sam got to his feet and sang the first words of "Silent Night." Everyone joined in, their voices rising in joyful sound. Matt thought he'd never heard anything so achingly beautiful, so...sincere.

As the last line died away, Sam walked over to the wall and turned out the light. The room went dim, but the outside lights cast a warm glow into the station's interior.

"It's nine o'clock," the ex-hippie announced. "I haven't been to bed this early in twenty years, but I'm more than ready to hit the hay."

His wife giggled. The two of them cuddled awkwardly on the hard bench, kissing and whispering.

Matt felt a pang of regret at seeing the closeness they shared, a closeness so sadly lacking in his own marriage. He glanced at his watch, certain that Pam would be home now, probably seething about the brief message he'd left. Nevertheless he wanted to talk to her. No, he corrected himself, he *needed* to talk to her.

Light from the window guided him to the far wall of the station, to the phones. Because it was still early, people continued to talk. He slipped his credit card through the slot and waited for the line to connect.

Pam answered on the first ring. "Hello." Her clipped tone told him she was angry, as he'd expected.

"It's Matt," he said.

"Matt?" She paused. "Matt?" she said again. "Where—"

"Merry Christmas, sweetheart," he whispered.

"How can you 'Merry Christmas' me with the kids screaming in my ear? Your parents are due any minute, and the house is a mess. The cat tipped over the Christmas tree and you're...you're..." She burst into tears.

"Pam," he said softly. "Honey, don't cry."

"I can't help it! I suppose you're in some posh hotel, ogling the cocktail waitress, while I'm here—"

"I'm not in any hotel."

"Then where are you?"

"A hundred-year-old train depot with..." Now it was his turn to pause. "With friends who were strangers not that long ago."

"A train depot?" She sniffled and sounded unsure.

"It's a long story and I'll tell you about it when I get home."

"You didn't phone all week."

"I know and I'm sorry, sweetheart, really sorry. It

was childish and silly of me to let our argument stand in the way of talking to you and the kids."

"You haven't called me sweetheart in a long time."

"Too long," Matt said. "I've done a lot of thinking these past few days, and once I'm home I want to talk to you about making some changes."

"I've been a terrible wife," she sobbed into the phone.

"Pam, you haven't. Now stop. I love you and you love me, and we're going to make it, understand?"

"Yes," she mumbled, her reply quavery with emotion.

"Listen, I want you to think about two things."

"Okay."

"First, I want to quit my job." Not until he said the words did Matt recognize how right it was to leave MicroChip. He should have known it when he was passed over for a promotion he'd earned. Being undervalued and underappreciated had cut into his self-confidence, and inevitably, his dissatisfaction with his job had affected his family life. He couldn't, wouldn't, allow that to continue.

"Quit your job?" Pam gasped.

"It isn't as bad as it sounds. I'm going to send out a couple of feelers right after New Year's. I've got a good reputation in the industry. I can get something else. The main thing is that I spend more time at home with you and the kids. It's unfair to have you chained down with all the responsibility for them and the house while I travel. I'm going to be looking for a sales position that won't take me away for more than a day at a time.''

"That sounds wonderful.''

"The other thing we need is a vacation, just the two of us. I've got vacation time coming, and it's been far too long since you and I got away without the kids.''

"I'd love that, Matt, more than anything.''

"How about a Caribbean cruise?'' he suggested.

"Yes... Oh, Matt, I love you so much and I've felt so awful about the way our marriage has been going.''

"Me, too. We'll talk about that some more. Maybe it wouldn't be such a bad idea to see a counselor, either.''

"Yes,'' she whispered.

Over the phone Matt heard a chorus of background shouts.

"Your parents just arrived,'' Pam told him.

"Let them wait. I want to say Merry Christmas to my wife.''

Eight

"Silent Night"

Cathy made up a small bed for herself using the blankets and pillows the VFW Women's Auxiliary had distributed. By all rights, she should be exhausted. She'd been up since dawn and the day had been filled with uncertainty and tension.

Instead, she lay with her eyes wide-open, mulling over the events of the past twenty-four hours. Apparently she wasn't the only one having difficulty sleeping. Matt, the sales rep, had carefully made his way across the darkened room and used the phone. It could be her imagination, but his steps seemed lighter on the return trip, as though his mood had improved. Cathy felt pleased for him. She'd lost patience with him earlier, and later...well, later, he'd proved to be an ally and a friend.

She'd witnessed more than one transformation today. The young sailor had been nervous and excited about this trip home; he'd chattered like a five-year-old when they'd first started out.

Then troubles developed, and he'd withdrawn into himself. But over the next few hours, Cathy had watched as Len recovered from his disappointment and frustration. Before the night was over he'd been an encouragement to others.

Nick and Kelly, the young couple with the new-born, were struggling to be good parents and still hold on to the closeness they'd once had in their marriage. Those two reminded Cathy of Ron and her about thirty years ago, after the birth of their first daughter. Eventually, like most couples, Nick and Kelly would learn to work together and ease gracefully into parenthood.

Sam and Louise had kept to themselves all day, offering no advice and little comment until Cathy shared her shortbread cookies. It was then that they'd kindly come forward and contributed their oranges. Later Sam had read the Christmas story from the Bible in a way that had stirred her beyond any Christmas Eve church service she'd ever attended.

She thought again of Matt McHugh. In the beginning he'd been quite disagreeable. Easily irritated, his few remarks cynical. One would assume that as a seasoned traveler he'd be better able to deal with frustrations of this sort. Unfortunately that wasn't the case until... Cathy couldn't put her finger on the precise moment she'd noticed the change in him. About the time they'd decorated the tree, she decided, when he'd opened his briefcase and started folding and clipping memos into paper snowflakes. She'd sensed a genuine enthusiasm in him from that point on.

Cathy had been just as affected by the unusual events of this Christmas Eve as her fellow passengers. That morning, when she'd phoned for a taxi in the middle of the snowstorm, she hadn't been looking forward to the trip. She'd dreaded it less, however, than spending the holiday alone in the house where she'd lived all those years with Ron.

She'd known Christmas would be difficult. After living first with the approach of death and then the aftermath of it, she'd anticipated nothing but pain and loneliness during the Christmas season. And she'd been right. But today, for the first time since standing over her husband's grave, she'd experienced what it meant to be alive. Sharing, encouraging, laughing. Damn, but it felt good.

"Are you awake?" Matt whispered from the bench directly across from her.

"Yes. You, too." She smiled at the obviousness of the comment.

"I just spoke to my wife." He sounded excited. "It was the first time we've connected all day."

"I imagine she was relieved to hear from you."

She saw his nod, and then he said the oddest thing.

"You loved your husband very much, didn't you?" he asked, sitting up and leaning toward her, bracing his elbows on his knees.

"Yes." Her voice wavered slightly, surprised as

she was by his question and the instant flash of pain it produced.

"I want my wife and me to have the same kind of relationship you did with your husband."

The comment touched her heart. "Thank you," she whispered, warmed by the praise of this stranger who'd become her friend. "How'd you know... I didn't mention Ron, I don't think."

"Ah, but you did," he said quietly, nestling against his pillow. "You told Kate about the dollhouse your husband built for his granddaughters. It was easy to read between the lines and...well, I could see this Christmas was difficult for you."

"It's better now," she whispered.

He sighed and curled up against the pillow before closing his eyes. "It's better for me, too."

"Merry Christmas, Matt."

"Merry Christmas, Cathy."

Len purposely waited until the depot was silent. The even rhythm of breathing told him that almost everyone was asleep. His watch said eleven-thirty, which made it ten-thirty in Rawhide. Amy had mentioned playing the piano at the rest home, and he'd waited until he was fairly confident she'd be home.

The phone card he'd paid for on base had long since expired, so he had to use his credit card. The transaction seemed loud enough to wake the entire room, but as far as Len could see, no one stirred.

When the line connected, the phone rang three times, three of the longest rings Len could ever remember hearing. He was about to give up hope when Amy answered.

"Hello." Her voice sounded breathless and excited at once.

"Merry Christmas, Amy," he said, speaking in a whisper for fear of disturbing the others.

"Len, Len, is that you?"

"It's me."

"Where are you?"

"The train depot," he said, wishing he had other news to give her.

"Still? Oh, Len, are you ever going to make it home?"

"And miss seeing my girl? Are you nuts? I'll walk from here to Rawhide if I have to."

"Oh, Len! I can't believe this is happening."

He'd felt much the same way himself most of the day, but somehow everything had changed after Mr. Kemper brought in the Christmas tree. And after the choir had come and the ladies had brought them a meal. And Sam had read the Christmas story...

In the beginning tempers had flared and folks were impatient and short with each other. Then the kind-hearted stationmaster had brought that bare sad-looking tree and placed it in the center of the room.

Someone had commented that the stupid tree wasn't worth the buck Kemper had paid for it.

Len had agreed. It'd taken a five-year-old child to teach them. The minute Kate had placed her hair bow on one sagging limb, the Christmas tree had been magically transformed into something beautiful. Not because of what they'd used to decorate its branches, but because of the effect it'd had on all of them, the way it had brought them together.

Everything had changed from then on. Suddenly they weren't strangers anymore. Suddenly it was a Christmas like those he'd enjoyed when he was a boy. He'd spent Christmas Eve with strangers who'd become so much more. Strangers who'd become family. Granted, it wasn't the same as if he'd spent Christmas Eve with Amy, but then he expected to be with her for the rest of his life.

"I'll be home before you know it," he promised.

"I'll be here," she whispered.

The line was quiet a moment while Len gathered his courage. He'd rather propose when he could look into her eyes and see her reaction as he said the words, but that wasn't possible. He didn't think he could wait any longer.

"Did you mean what you said earlier?" he asked. "Do you really love me, Amy Sue?"

"Yes," she admitted as though confessing to a fault. "I…I probably shouldn't have said it."

"Why not?" he asked, raising his voice before he could stop himself.

"Because…well, because we've never talked about our feelings and—"

"I love you, too, Amy."

She didn't say anything for so long Len feared they'd been disconnected.

"Amy?"

"I'm here."

He could tell from the tremble in her voice that she was close to tears. "Amy, listen, I never intended it to happen like this, but then life doesn't always go the way we plan it. I decided to come home for another reason besides spending Christmas with my family."

"What?"

"I was hoping…" Despite rehearsing his proposal, he was tongue-tied and nervous.

"You were hoping…" she encouraged.

"To talk to you about something important."

"Yes?"

"About the two of us." He continued to improvise, forgetting the carefully worded proposal he'd practiced a hundred times. "I was thinking you and I…that is, if you were interested…that maybe we should get married."

There was a silence that seemed to go on and on.

"Married," she finally repeated, sounding stunned.

Len's hand tightened around the telephone receiver. His nerves were stretched to the limit. "Say something," he pleaded, all the while wondering if it was possible to get a refund on the diamond if she refused him. His heart sank to his knees; he hadn't considered Amy's refusal. In his arrogance he'd assumed she'd scream with delight, maybe even cry a little. The last thing he'd anticipated was no response.

"Amy?" he asked, humble now, wondering how he could have made such a mistake in judgment. He'd noted the reserve in her recently, the fact that he hadn't gotten a letter in almost two weeks. Other things didn't add up, either, but he'd pushed his concerns aside each time he spoke with her—although of course their phone calls had been less frequent lately. But whenever he managed to call she'd always sounded so glad to hear from him.

"Is there someone else?" he demanded, his pride rescuing him. "Is that it?"

"Oh, Len, how can you think such a thing?"

"Then what's it to be?" A proposal was a straightforward enough question. "Yes or no?"

"Who told you?"

"Told me?" he echoed. "Told me what?"

"About the baby."

Nine

"Baby?" Len's knees went weak and to remain upright he braced his shoulder against the wall.

"Who told you?" Amy repeated.

"No one…" Len's thoughts twisted around in his mind until he was convinced he'd misunderstood her. "To make sure I understand what's happening here, I need to ask you something. Are you telling me you're pregnant?"

"Yes."

"Don't you think you should've mentioned this before now?" he demanded, not caring who heard him. "You must be at least three months along."

"Three and a half… I love you, Len, but you've never said how you felt about me. I didn't want you to feel obligated to marry me. My dad married my mother because she was pregnant and the marriage was a disaster. I refuse to repeat my mother's mistakes, although I certainly seem to have started out on the same path."

"Amy, listen, I swear I didn't know about the baby. No one told me a damn thing." He took a deep breath. "As for you being like your mom...this is different. I love you. I want us to get married. I wanted it even before I knew about the baby." It hurt to think Amy had held back, not telling him she was pregnant. "Who else knows?"

"Jenny."

"You'd tell your best friend before you'd tell me?" he said, hardly able to believe his ears.

"Why'd you ask me to marry you?" she returned, equally insistent. "Is it just because of the baby?"

"No... I already told you that. Isn't loving you and wanting to spend the rest of my life with you reason enough?"

"Yes," she whispered, whimpering now. "It's more than enough."

"Listen, Amy. I want to be with you. And I want my baby. We're getting married, understand? Soon, too, next week if it can be arranged, and when I go back to Maine, I'm going to ask for married housing. Next month I'll come down and get you."

"Len..."

That was the reason she'd asked if she was just "his girl in Rawhide." He hated the thought of her worrying and fretting all these weeks, wondering how he'd react once he learned the truth.

"You said you love me. Are you taking that back now?" he asked.

"No…"

"I love you. I knew it after my last visit home. I should have said something then. I regret now that I didn't." Then, remembering how he didn't enjoy having his life dictated to him, he asked again, "Will you marry me, Amy?"

Her hesitation was only momentary this time. "Yes, Len, oh, yes."

He could hear her sob softly in the background.

"I knew tonight would be special," she murmured.

"How's that?" Len's mind continued to spin with Amy's news, but it wasn't unwelcome. He was ready to be a husband and had always loved children. His own parents had been wonderful and he was determined to be a good husband and father himself.

"Mr. Danbar came out of his room tonight when I sat down at the piano," Amy told him.

Len could only vaguely recall the man's name. "Mr. Danbar?"

"He's the one who hasn't spoken a word since his wife died three years ago. The man I eat my lunch with every day. I'm the one who does all the talking, but that's all right."

"He came out of his room?" This was big news, Len realized. He remembered now that Amy had written to him about the older gentleman.

"His wife used to play the piano and when he heard the music, he climbed out of bed and came into the recreation room. He sat down on the bench beside me and smiled. Oh, Len, it was the most amazing thing.''

His wife-to-be was pretty darn amazing herself, he thought proudly. She could coax a lonely old man from his room and brighten his life with her music and kindness. Len meant what he'd said, about their marrying as soon as possible. Their marriage would be a strong one, based on love and mutual respect.

He felt like the luckiest man alive.

''Are you awake?'' Nick whispered to Kelly in the dead of night. He thought he'd heard her stir and realized they were both accustomed to Brittany waking and needing to be fed around this time.

Nick had been wide-awake for the better part of an hour. Sleeping upright with his head propped against the wall had been awkward, but he'd managed to get some rest. It helped to have his arm around Kelly and hold her close to his side. They hadn't held each other nearly enough lately, but that was something he hoped to remedy.

In response to his question, Kelly yawned. ''What time is it?''

''About two.''

''Already?'' His wife smothered a second yawn. ''How's Brittany?''

''Better than either of us.''

Nick grinned into the darkness and gently squeezed her shoulder.

"I never thought we'd spend our first Christmas as parents stuck in some train depot," Kelly said, her words barely audible.

"Me, neither."

"It hasn't been so bad."

Nick pressed his face into her hair and inhaled, delighting in her warm female scent. He loved Kelly and Brittany more than he'd thought it was possible to love anyone. More than it seemed reasonable for any human heart to love. Little in his life had come easy, and this parenting business might well be his greatest challenge yet. But his struggles had taught him to appreciate what he did have. Tonight, Christmas Eve, had taught him to *recognize* what he had.

He'd considered the trip home to Georgia unnecessary, but Kelly had wanted to introduce Brittany to her grandparents. Besides, traveling in winter was a mistake, he'd told her over and over. In the end he'd agreed only because Kelly had wanted it so badly. He hadn't been gracious about it, and when troubles arose, it was all he could do not to leap up and tell her how right he'd been.

Nick felt differently now. Being with these people on Christmas Eve hadn't been a mistake at all. Nor was taking Brittany to meet her extended family. They needed each other. He'd stood alone most of his life, but he wasn't alone anymore. He had a wife and daughter. Family. And friends.

More friends than he'd realized.

* * *

At six o'clock Christmas morning, Clayton Kemper received word that the tracks had been repaired. He hurriedly dressed and rushed down to the train depot, not sure what he'd find. It came as a pleasant surprise to discover everyone waking up in a good mood, grateful to hear his news. While the travelers stretched and yawned, Clayton put on a pot of coffee, then dragged out the phone book and called the hotels in town to alert the passengers there that the tracks had been repaired.

"I don't imagine this will be a Christmas you'll soon forget," Clayton said as he led the small band from the depot to the train. The engine hummed, ready to race down the tracks toward Boston.

Mrs. Norris was the first to board. She smiled as she placed her hand in his. "Thank you again for all your kindness, Mr. Kemper. And Merry Christmas."

"I was glad I could help," he said as she climbed onto the train.

The couple with the baby followed, along with the young navy man who lugged his own bag as well as the infant seat. It never ceased to amaze Clayton that one baby could need this much equipment. Time was, a bottle or two and a few diapers would suffice. These days it took the mother and two full-grown men to cart everything in. Clayton was pleased to see that the couple had struck up a friendship with the sailor. They certainly seemed to have a great deal to talk about.

The sales rep boarded next, after helping an elderly black couple with their luggage. This was the man who'd spent a large portion of the day before scowling and muttering under his breath. Kemper didn't know what had happened to him, but this morning the man grinned from ear to ear and was about as helpful as they come.

"We appreciate everything you did for us, Kemper," he said as he made his way into the train.

Five-year-old Kate bounced onto the first step and told Clayton, "Santa came last night and dropped off a present for me and Charles."

"Did he now?" Clayton asked, catching Elise Jones's eyes.

"Indeed he did," Elise said with a wide smile.

Apparently the adults had arranged something for the children. Clayton was glad to hear it. He wished he'd been able to do more himself, but he had his own family and plenty of obligations. It was a sad case when the railroad had to put people up in a depot for the night, especially when that night happened to be Christmas Eve.

He waited until everyone was on board before he stepped away from the train. Glancing inside the compartment, he watched fascinated as the group of once-cantankerous travelers cheerfully teased one another. Anyone looking at them would assume they were lifelong friends, even family.

Was it possible, Clayton wondered, that this small

band of strangers had discovered the true meaning of Christmas? Learned it in a train depot late on Christmas Eve in the middle of a snowstorm?

The question seemed to answer itself.

SHIRLEY, GOODNESS
AND MERCY

To my St. Simons Island, Georgia, friends

Becky and Hank Wyrick
Hilaire Bauer
Jackie Randall
and
Phillip DePoy

One

Greg Bennett had always hated Christmas.

He'd never believed in "goodwill toward men" and all that other sentimental garbage. Christmas in the city—any city—was the epitome of commercialism, and San Francisco was no exception. Here it was, barely December, and department-store windows had been filled with automated elves and tinsel-hung Christmas trees since before Thanksgiving!

Most annoying, in Greg's opinion, was the hustle and bustle of holiday shoppers, all of whom seemed to be unnaturally cheerful. That only made his own mood worse.

He wouldn't be in the city at all if he wasn't desperately in need of a bank loan. Without it, he'd be forced to lay off what remained of his crew by the end of the year. He'd have to close the winery's doors. His vines—and literally decades of work—had been wiped out by fan leaf disease, devastating the future of his vineyard and crippling him financially.

He'd spent the morning visiting one financial institution after another. Like a number of other growers, he'd applied at the small-town banks in the Napa Valley and been unsuccessful. His wasn't the only vineyard destroyed by the disease—although, for reasons no one really understood, certain vineyards had been spared the blight. For a while there'd been talk of low-interest loans from the federal government, but they hadn't materialized. Apparently the ruin hadn't been thorough enough to warrant financial assistance. For Greg that news definitely fell into the category of cold comfort.

It left him in a dilemma. No loan—no replanted vines. Without the vines there would be no grapes, without the grapes, no wine, and without the winery, no Gregory Bennett.

What he needed after a morning such as this, he decided, was a good stiff drink and the company of a charming female companion, someone who could help him forget his current troubles. He walked into the St. Francis, the elegant San Francisco hotel, and found himself facing a twenty-foot Christmas tree decorated with huge gold balls and plush red velvet bows. Disgusted, he looked away and hurried toward the bar.

The bartender seemed to sense his urgency. "What can I get you?" he asked promptly. He wore a name tag that identified him as Don.

Greg sat down on a stool. "Get me a martini," he said. If it hadn't been so early in the day, he would have asked for a double, but it was barely noon and he still had to drive home. He didn't feel any compelling reason to return. The house, along with everything else in his life, was empty. Oh, the furniture was all there—Tess hadn't taken that—but he was alone, more alone than he could ever remember being.

Tess, his third and greediest wife, had left him six months earlier. The attorneys were fighting out the details of their divorce, and at three hundred dollars an hour, neither lawyer had much incentive to rush into court.

Nevertheless, Tess was gone. He silently toasted eliminating her from his life and vowed not to make the mistake of marrying again. Three wives was surely sufficient evidence that he wasn't the stay-married kind.

Yet he missed Tess, he mused with some regret—and surprise. Well, maybe not Tess exactly, but a warm body in his bed. By his side. Even at the time, he'd known it was foolish to marry her. He certainly *should* have known, after the messy end of his second marriage. His first had lasted ten years, and he'd split with Jacquie over... Hell if he could remember. Something stupid. It'd always been something stupid.

"You out shopping?" Don the bartender asked as he delivered a bowl of peanuts.

Greg snorted. "Not on your life."

The younger man smiled knowingly. "Ah, you're one of those."

"You mean someone who's got common sense.

What is it with people and Christmas? Normal, sane human beings become sentimental idiots.'' A year ago, when he and Tess had been married less than eighteen months, she'd made it clear she expected diamonds for Christmas. Lots of them. She'd wanted him to make her the envy of her friends. That was what he got for marrying a woman nineteen years his junior. A pretty blonde with a figure that could stop traffic. Next time around he'd simply move the woman into his house and send her packing when he grew bored with her. No more marriages—not for him. He didn't need any more legal entanglements.

Just then a blond beauty entered the bar, and Greg did a double take. For half a heartbeat, he thought it was Tess. Thankfully he was wrong. Blond, beautiful and probably a bitch. The last part didn't bother him, though—especially now, when he could use a little distraction. He'd be sixty-one his next birthday, but he was trim and fit, and still had all his hair—gone mostly gray, what people called "distinguished." In fact, he could easily pass for ten years younger. His good looks had taken him a long way in this world, and he'd worked hard to maintain a youthful appearance.

"Welcome," he greeted her, swerving around on his stool to give her his full attention.

"Hello."

Her answering smile told him she wasn't averse to his company. Yes, she might well provide a distraction. If everything worked out, he might stay in town overnight. Considering the morning he'd had, he deserved a little comfort. He wasn't interested in anything serious—just a light flirtation to take his mind off his troubles, a dalliance to momentarily distract him.

"Are you meeting someone?" Greg asked.

"Not really," she said, her voice sultry and deep.

Greg noted the packages. "Been shopping, I see."

She nodded, and when the bartender walked over to her table, Greg said, "Put it on my tab."

"Thanks," she said in that same sultry voice. He was even more impressed when she asked for a glass of Bennett Wine. A pinot noir.

He slipped off the stool and approached her table. "I'm Greg."

"Cherry Adams."

He liked her name; it suited her. "Do you mind if I join you?"

"Go ahead. Why not?"

The day was already looking brighter. He pulled out a chair and sat down. They made small talk for a few minutes, exchanged pleasantries. He didn't mention his last name because he didn't want her to make the connection and have their conversation weighed down by the problems at Bennett Wines. However, it soon became clear that she was knowledgeable about wine—and very flattering about his 1996 pinot noir. Tess had been an idiot on the subject, despite being married to the owner of a winery. She didn't know the difference between chablis and chardonnay. And she never did understand why he couldn't call his own sparkling wine champagne, no matter how many times he told her the name could only be used for sparkling wines from the Champagne region of France.

After another glass of wine for her and a second martini for him, Greg suggested lunch. Cherry hesitated and gazed down at her hands. "Sorry, but I've got a nail appointment."

"You could cancel it," Greg suggested, trying to hint that they could find more entertaining ways to occupy themselves. He didn't want her to think he was being pushy. Later, after lunch, he'd surprise her and announce who he really was. He was pleased—no, delighted—by her interest in him, particularly because she didn't know he was the man responsible for the wine she'd described as "exquisite." He grinned; wait till he told her. Cherry's interest proved what he'd been telling himself ever since Tess had walked out on him. He was still young, still vital, still sexy.

That was when it happened.

The look that crossed Cherry's face conveyed her thoughts as clearly as if she'd said them aloud. She wasn't interested. Oh, sure, he was good for a few drinks, especially since he was buying. Good for an hour of conversation. But that was all.

"I really do have to go," Cherry said as she

reached for her shopping bags. "My nails are a mess. Thanks for the, uh, company and the wine, though."

"Don't mention it," Greg muttered, watching her leave. He was still reeling from the blow to his pride.

Soon afterward, he left, too. He'd never been one to take rejection well, mainly because he'd had so little experience of it.

After two martinis he knew he wasn't in any condition to drive. So he left his car in the lot and started to walk. With no destination in mind, he wandered down the crowded street, trying to keep his distance from all those happy little shoppers. His stomach growled and his head hurt, but not nearly as much as his ego. Every time he thought about the look on Cherry's face, he cringed. Okay, okay, she'd been too young. At a guess he'd say she was no more than thirty.

However, Greg knew a dozen women her age who would leap at the opportunity to spend a day and a night with him. He was suave, sophisticated and rich. Not as rich as he'd once been—would be again, as soon as he got this latest mess straightened out. *If* he got it straightened out. The truth was, he stood on the brink of losing everything.

Desperate to escape his dark thoughts, he began to walk at a brisker pace. He made an effort not to think, not to acknowledge his fears and worries, concentrating, instead, on the movement of his feet, the rhythm of his breath. He turned corner after corner

and eventually found himself on a side street dominated by an imposing brick church.

He paused in front of it. A church. Now that was
a laugh. He remembered how his mother had dragged
him and his brother, Phil, to service every Sunday.
He'd even attended services while he was in college.
But he hadn't darkened the door of a church
since…Catherine.

She'd been his sweetheart, his *lover,* during college—until he'd broken it off. No, abandoned her.
That was a more honest description of what he'd
done. The years had numbed his guilt, and he rarely
thought of her anymore. Funny how a relationship
that had ended more than thirty-five years ago could
suddenly rise up to haunt him. He'd been a senior the
last time he'd seen Catherine. They'd been madly in
love. Then she'd told him she was pregnant and Greg
had panicked. About to graduate, about to start his
life, he'd done what had seemed sensible at the time;
he'd fled.

Unable to face her, he'd written Catherine a letter
and told her he was leaving. She should do whatever
she wanted about the baby. It'd been cowardly of
him, but he was just a kid back then; he'd long since
stopped berating himself over it. He'd never heard
from her again. He didn't know what she'd done
about the baby. Didn't want to know. Abortions
hadn't been legal at the time, but there were ways of
getting rid of an unwanted pregnancy even then. His

mother hadn't ever learned why his relationship with Catherine had ended, but Phil knew. That was the beginning of the estrangement between Greg and his brother.

Almost without realizing it, Greg began to move up the church steps. He blamed it on the throng of shoppers crowding in around him. All he wanted was a few moments of peace and quiet. A chance to think.

He hesitated on the top step. He didn't belong in a church, not the way he'd lived. And yet...

His life was empty and he was old enough to recognize that. But at sixty, it was a bit late. For most of his adult life, he'd followed the path of least resistance, put his own interests above those of other people. He'd believed that was the basis of prosperity, of success. Deserting Catherine was where it had started.

She'd been the first of his regrets. Matthias was the second. And then his mother...

Matthias Jamison was his father's cousin and an employee at the winery. Greg's parents had divorced when he was in high school, and he and Phil had spent summers with their father at the vineyard. Although the younger of the two, Greg was the one who'd been drawn to the family business. He'd spent hour after hour there, learning everything he could about wine and wine making.

Ten years his senior, Matthias had taken Greg under his wing. What John Bennett didn't teach Greg about wine making, Matthias did. His father had also insisted Greg get a business degree, and he'd been right. Several years later, when he died, Greg bought out Phil's half to become sole owner and worked with Matthias operating the winery.

The wine had always been good. What the business needed was an aggressive advertising campaign. People couldn't order the Bennett label if they'd never heard of it. The difficulty with Greg's ideas was the huge financial investment they demanded. Commissioning sophisticated full-page ads and placing them in upscale food magazines, attending wine expositions throughout the world—it had all cost money. He'd taken a gamble, which was just starting to pay off when Matthias came to him, needing a loan.

Mary, Matthias's wife of many years, had developed a rare form of blood cancer. The experimental drug that might save her life wasn't covered by their health insurance. The cost of the medication was threatening to bankrupt Matthias; his savings were gone and no bank would lend him money. He'd asked Greg for help. After everything the older man had done for him and for his family, Greg knew he owed Matthias that and more.

The decision had been agonizing. Bennett Wines was just beginning to gain recognition; sales had doubled and tripled. But Greg's plans were bigger than that. He'd wanted to help Matthias, but there was no guarantee the treatment would be effective. So he'd turned Matthias down. Mary had died a few months later, when conventional treatments failed, and a bitter Matthias had left Bennett Wines and moved to Washington state.

Generally Greg didn't encourage friendships. He tended to believe that friends took advantage of you, that they resented your success. It was every man for himself, in Greg's view. Still, Matthias had been the best friend he'd ever had. Because of what happened, the two men hadn't spoken in fifteen years.

Greg could have used Matthias's expertise in dealing with the blight that had struck his vines, but he was too proud to give him the opportunity to slam the door in his face. To refuse him the way he'd refused Matthias all those years ago.

No, Greg definitely wasn't church material. Whatever had possessed him to think he should go into this place, seek solace here, he couldn't fathom.

He was about to turn away when he noticed that the church doors were wide open. Had they been open all this time? He supposed they must have been. It was almost as if he was being invited inside.... He shook his head, wondering where *that* ridiculous thought had come from. Nevertheless, he slowly walked in.

The interior was dim and his eyes took a moment to adjust. He saw that the sanctuary was huge, with two rows of pews facing a wide altar. Even the church was decorated for the holidays. Pots of red and white poinsettias were arranged on the altar, and a row of gaily decorated Christmas trees stood behind it. A large cross hung suspended from the ceiling.

An organ sat off to one side, along with a sectioned space for the choir. Greg hadn't stopped to notice which denomination this church was. Nor did he care.

Although his mother had been an ardent church-goer, Greg had hated it, found it meaningless. But Phil seemed to eat this religious stuff up, just like their mother had.

"Okay," Greg said aloud. None of this whispering business for him. "The door was open. I came inside. You want me to tell you I made a mess of my life? Fine, I screwed up. I could've done better. Is that what you were waiting to hear? Is that what you wanted me to say? I said it. Are you happy now?"

His words reverberated, causing him to retreat a step.

And as he did, his life suddenly overwhelmed him. His failures, his shortcomings, his mistakes came roaring at him like an avalanche, jerking him off his feet. He seemed to tumble backward through the years. The force of it was too much and he slumped into a pew, the weight of his past impossible to bear. He leaned forward and buried his face in his hands.

"Can you forgive me, Mama?" he whispered brokenly. "Is there any way I can make up for what I did—not being there for you? When you needed me..."

He deserved every rotten thing that was happening

to him. If he couldn't get a loan, if he lost the winery, it would be what he deserved. All of it.

Greg wouldn't have recognized his words as a prayer. But, they wove their way upward, past the church altar, past the suspended crucifix, toward the bell tower and church steeple. Once free of the building, they flew heavenward, through the clouds and beyond the sky, landing with a crash on the cluttered desk of the Archangel Gabriel.

"Well, well," the archangel said, a little surprised and more than a little pleased. "What do we have here?"

Two

The Archangel Gabriel arched his white brows as he reviewed Greg Bennett's file. A very thick file. "Well, it's about time," he muttered, and dutifully recorded the prayer request.

"I certainly agree with you there," a soft female voice murmured in response.

Gabriel didn't have to look up to see who'd joined him. That angelic voice was all too familiar. Shirley was visiting, and where Shirley was, Goodness and Mercy were sure to follow. His three favorite troublemakers—heaven help him. Without having to ask, he knew what she wanted. The trio had been pestering him for three years about a return trip to earth.

"Hello, Shirley," Gabriel said without much enthusiasm. The truth was, he'd always been partial to Shirley, Goodness and Mercy, although he dared not let it show. Their escapades on earth were notorious in the corridors of paradise and had created an uproar on more than one occasion.

"We've decided you seem frazzled," Goodness

said, popping up next to her friend. She rested her arms on Gabriel's desk, studying him avidly.

"Overworked," Mercy agreed, appearing beside the other two.

"And we're here to help." Shirley walked around the front of his desk and gave him a pitying look.

"We feel your pain," Goodness told him.

If she hadn't sounded so sincere, Gabriel would have laughed outright. He was still tempted to tell her to cut the psychobabble, but knew that wouldn't do any good. As it was, he sighed and leaned back in his chair.

"So—what *can* we do to help?" Mercy inquired with a serenity few would question.

"Help?" he asked. "You can help me most by participating in the heavenly host again this year."

"We've already done that for three years," Goodness complained with a slight pout, crossing her arms. "It's just no fun to be one in a cast of thousands."

"We want to go back to earth," Shirley explained. Of the three, she was the most plainspoken. Gabriel knew he could count on her to tell him the truth. She did her utmost to keep the other two in line, but could only hold out for so long before she succumbed to temptation herself.

"I love humans," Goodness said, hands clasped as she gazed longingly toward earth.

"Me, too," Mercy was quick to add. "Where else

in the universe would anyone assume God is dead and Elvis is alive?''

Gabriel successfully hid a smile. ''Even with the best of intentions, you three have never been able to keep your wings to yourselves.''

''True.'' Shirley nodded in agreement. ''But remember we're angels, not saints.''

''All the more reason to make you stay in heaven where you belong,'' Gabriel argued.

The objections came fast and furious.

''But you need us this year!''

''More than ever, Gabriel. You've got far more work than you can handle!''

''You're overburdened!''

True enough. As always, Christmas was his busiest time of year, and Gabriel's desk was flooded with thousands upon thousands of prayer requests. No denying it, human beings were the most difficult of God's subjects. Obtuse, demanding and contrary. Many of them flung prayer requests at heaven without once considering that humans played a role in solving their own problems. The hard part was getting them to recognize that they had lessons to learn before their prayer requests could be granted. God-directed solutions often came from within themselves. Gabriel's task, with the help of his other prayer ambassadors, was to show these proud stubborn creatures the way.

''Do you have any requests from children?'' Shirley asked. As a former guardian angel, she enjoyed working with youngsters the most.

"Anyone in need of a little Mercy?" Mercy prodded.

"Any good faithful souls who could use a bit of angelic guidance?" Goodness asked.

"Here," Gabriel said abruptly as he shoved Greg Bennett's prayer request at them.

Gabriel didn't know what had possessed him. Frustration, perhaps. Then again, it could have been something far more powerful. It could have been the very hand of God. "This request will require all three of you. Read it over, do your homework and get back to me. You might decide that singing with the heavenly host doesn't sound so bad, after all."

He grinned sheepishly as they fluttered away, eager to discover everything they could about this sad human and the sorry mess he'd made of his life.

In truth Gabriel half expected they'd choose to return to the heavenly choir; if they did he wouldn't blame them. Greg Bennett's case would be a challenge for the most experienced prayer ambassadors— let alone these three. Once Shirley, Goodness and Mercy had the opportunity to read his file, they were bound to see that.

The trio gathered around the file detailing the life of Greg Bennett. Shirley noted that their excited chatter had quickly died down as they read. The oldest and most mature, she could see through Gabriel's ploy. The archangel expected them to give up before they started. To tell him how right he was and scurry back to choir practice. In light of what she'd learned about Greg Bennett, perhaps that would be for the best.

"Oh, my," Goodness whispered. "He abandoned his college sweetheart when she was pregnant."

"Deserted his best friend in his hour of need."

"Look what he did to his own *mother!*"

"To his mother?"

Shirley nodded. "Greg Bennett is a—"

"Scumbag," Mercy supplied.

"He's arrogant."

"Selfish."

"And conceited."

"It's going to take a whole bunch of miracles to whip this poor boy into shape."

Shirley had no argument there. "I'm afraid Greg Bennett is more than any of us could handle," she said sadly.

Goodness and Mercy glanced at each other. "She's joking, isn't she?"

"No, I'm not," Shirley said on a disparaging note. "You read for yourself what kind of man he is. Frankly, I feel someone else, someone who's got more experience with humans and their frailties, would be better equipped to deal with the likes of Mr. Bennett."

"Oh, fiddlesticks!" Goodness cried.

"We can do it," Mercy contended with considerably more confidence than the success of her earlier exploits might have warranted.

"We all know Gabriel did this on purpose," Goodness said. Apparently she hadn't been fooled, either. "He assumed that once we see what a mess Greg's made of his life, we'll figure it's hopeless and slink back to the choir. Well, I, for one, have no intention of spending another Christmas singing my lungs out over the fields of Bethlehem. To be so close to earth and yet so far…"

Mercy giggled but appeared to be in full agreement. "Come on, Shirley, this is our one and only chance to return to earth. Okay, so you're right. Greg Bennett isn't exactly a believer in God's love, but God does love him. Heaven knows he needs help."

Shirley was adamant. "More than we can give him."

"Don't be such a pessimist," Goodness chided. "If nothing else, we can steer him in the right direction."

"San Francisco," Mercy said, tapping her cheek. "There are ships in San Francisco, aren't there?"

Shirley could already see trouble brewing. "You've got to promise to stay away from the shipyard," she said heatedly. It'd taken them years to live down what had happened at the Bremerton Naval Shipyard in Washington state. The news crew that covered the repositioning of two aircraft carriers might as well have been reporting directly to heaven, what with all the attention the incident had received.

"Okay, I promise, no shipyard," Mercy said. Shirley was appeased until she thought she saw her fellow angel wink at Goodness. Oh, my, if they took the Bennett case, then this was going to be some Christmas. On the other hand…

"Where are you headed?" Goodness called out when Shirley broke away.

"I'm going back to tell Gabriel we'll take the job. Just don't make me sorry I agreed to this."

"Would we do that?" Mercy asked, the picture of angelic innocence.

Shirley had a very good reason for feeling skeptical, but an even better reason for tackling this stint on earth. She wanted out of the choir as much as her two friends did. A human, even one who happened to have more than his share of frailties, wasn't going to stop her.

"Hi, Dad!" Michael Thorpe bounded enthusiastically into the hospital clinic, his eyes sparkling.

Dr. Edward Thorpe looked up from the chart he was reading and smiled at the sight of his son. His wife, Janice, five months pregnant, hurried to keep up with the energetic boy.

The six-year-old raced into his arms and Edward lifted him high above his head. Seeing his own healthy happy son was exactly what he needed. Much

of his morning had been spent with another youngster, Tanner Westley, who was ten and suffering from
a rare form of leukemia. Edward was an oncologist
who specialized in childhood cancers; his work had
recently garnered the interest of the *San Francisco
Herald.* Just today, a reporter had interviewed him for
a piece the paper was running on the urgent need for
bone-marrow donors. The story would include a photograph of Tanner. Most members of the public didn't
seem to understand that they had the opportunity to
save lives by testing to become donors. The only
thing required at this stage was a simple blood test.
The article would make a strongly worded plea for
bone-marrow donors to help children such as Tanner.

The reporter felt the timing was good. People
seemed more generous with their time and money
over the Christmas period. Edward hoped they'd be
equally giving about submitting to a blood test.

"Hello, darling," his wife said.

"Is it lunchtime already?" With the interview and
Tanner Westley's additional tests, his morning had
flown.

Janice glanced at her watch. "Actually, we're
late."

"Mom and I were shopping." Michael rolled his
eyes as if to say how much that had bored him. Edward hid a smile. An intolerance for shopping was
something he had in common with his son.

"Can you still join us for lunch?" Janice asked.

Now it was Edward's turn to glance at his watch. "If you don't mind eating in the cafeteria." He needed to be within a few minutes of Tanner, who was starting a new chemotherapy session today.

"We can eat in the cafeteria, can't we, Mom?" Michael tugged at his mother's arm. "Their ice-cream machine is way cool."

"Okay—I'm convinced," Janice responded good-naturedly as the three of them headed toward the elevator.

"Why are we here?" Goodness demanded, her voice unnaturally high. "You *know* I don't like hospitals."

"I didn't bring us here. Shirley did."

"Would you two stop it?" Shirley sighed in exasperation. Goodness and Mercy were enough to try the patience of a saint, let alone another angel. "That's Greg Bennett's son."

"Which one?"

"The cancer specialist," Shirley said, thinking it should have been obvious.

"You mean he's Catherine's child?"

"Right." It was Gabriel who'd directed her to the hospital, but she hadn't told the others that. As far as she was concerned, they would receive information strictly on a need-to-know basis. It was safer that way.

"But he's wonderful!"

"Unlike his birth father," Goodness said under her breath.

Shirley agreed completely. "Greg Bennett broke Catherine's heart, you know." The file had told her that, and ever since, she'd found it a struggle to care in the slightest about Greg and his vineyard.

"She loved him deeply," Mercy added, shaking her head. "When Greg turned his back on her, she was devastated."

"Then she gave birth to Edward and raised him on her own, and had trouble trusting men again for a very long time."

"She didn't marry until Edward was nearly eight." Shirley recounted the facts as she remembered them. "But she's very happy now...."

"Does she have other children?"

"A daughter, who's a child psychologist," Shirley supplied. "They meet every Friday for lunch on Fisherman's Wharf."

"That's on the waterfront, isn't it?" Mercy brightened.

Shirley cast her fellow angel a quelling look. She didn't want to say it, but Mercy's obsession with ships was beginning to bother her. Oh, my, she didn't know how she was going to get through this holiday season with Goodness and Mercy and still have any kind of effect on Greg Bennett. As much fun as it was to enjoy the things of this earth, they were on an important mission and didn't have time to get side-tracked.

"Meanwhile, Greg has had three wives and each one of them looks exactly like Catherine," Goodness pointed out.

Shirley hadn't recognized that, but as soon as Goodness made the observation, she knew it was true. "Only he doesn't see there's a pattern here," she murmured.

"He hasn't opened his eyes wide enough to see it," Goodness said.

"Yet." Mercy crossed her arms in a determined way that seemed to suggest she'd take great delight in telling him.

"Yet?" Shirley raised her eyebrows in warning, but continued her summary of Greg's failings. "His only child, a son he deserted before he was born, grew up to become a noted cancer specialist, while Greg has squandered his life on wine and women."

"Yes, and while he was trying to pick up some blond babe in a fancy bar, Edward was treating a ten-year-old leukemia patient," Mercy said in a scornful voice.

Goodness grew quiet, which was always a danger-ous sign.

"What are you thinking?" Shirley asked her.

"I'm thinking about Catherine," Goodness confessed.

"He hasn't seen her since college," Shirley put in.

"But it seems to me that Greg's been searching for her in every woman he's met," Goodness said thoughtfully.

"Certainly every woman he marries," Mercy added, not concealing her disgust.

"And?" Shirley prodded. "What's your point, Goodness?"

"Well…perhaps we should do something to help make it happen."

"What do you mean?"

"Well, if he's looking for Catherine, which he *seems* to be doing, we can make sure he finds her. He should see what she's done with her life, how happy she is…"

"Goodness, I don't think that's such a good idea," Shirley protested. "You know the rules as well as I do, and we're not supposed to interfere in human lives."

"Who said anything about interfering?"

"There isn't any rule against sending humans in a particular direction, is there?" Mercy asked.

"No, but…" Shirley began. Goodness and Mercy, however, had disappeared before the words left her lips.

Oh, dear. Already it was starting. Already she'd lost control.

Shirley raced after the other two, hoping she could stop them in time.

Three

Greg had remained in the church longer than he'd intended. He felt a little foolish sitting there in that quiet darkened place all alone. It was almost as if…as if he was waiting for something to happen. Or for someone to appear and speak to him—which, of course, was ridiculous. God was hardly going to drop down and have a heart-to-heart with someone like him.

Other than that unaccountable feeling of anticipation, nothing out of the ordinary had occurred during the time he'd been in this church. Nevertheless, the experience had calmed him. For that half hour, Greg was able to set his troubles aside. He'd never been one to dwell on the negatives; it was far easier to push his regrets and worries from his mind, pretend they didn't exist. Anyway, he'd always managed to surmount his business problems, even when the vineyard had suffered from other disasters—flooding or frost or even fire.

Only this time he had a gut feeling that there wasn't going to be any last-minute rescue. This one was different. If some kind of solution didn't turn up soon, he was going to lose everything.

At sixty he was too old to start over.

After he left the church, he began walking again, his thoughts heavy. It probably wasn't a good idea to drive yet, so he aimlessly wandered the streets. He considered the few options he had. He could declare bankruptcy. Or he could throw himself on his brother's mercy. Phil had become a vice president of Pacific Union, one of the largest banks in the state. He could certainly pull strings to help Greg secure a loan.

But they hadn't spoken since their mother's death. Greg didn't blame Phil for hating him, especially after what he'd done. Another regret. Another person who'd needed him—another person he'd failed. His own mother.

A sick feeling settled over him. He increased his pace as if he could outdistance his guilt. His mother might have forgiven him, but his brother hadn't. Their quarrel following the funeral had ended any chance Greg might have had of receiving Phil's help now.

Although he wasn't hungry, Greg decided to find some lunch. With food in his stomach to cut the effects of the alcohol, he could safely drive, and empty though it was, home had begun to seem mighty appealing.

He could buy a cup of chowder or a seafood sandwich along Fisherman's Wharf, so he hurried downhill toward the waterfront, his pace filled with sudden purpose. The wind was cold and brisk, and he gathered his coat around him as he neared the wharf. What on earth were all these people doing here? No doubt spending their money on useless junk for Christmas. Grumbling, he wove his way through the crowds toward the closest fish bar.

"There she is," Goodness whispered, pressing her face against the restaurant window.

"You found her?" Mercy sounded incredulous as she peered in the window, too. "Oh, my, Catherine really is lovely."

Shirley couldn't resist. She cupped her hands about her face and gazed through the smudged glass, too.

"Her daughter looks exactly like her," Mercy said.

Her friends were right, Shirley thought. Catherine was a classic beauty who carried herself with grace and elegance. Her daughter, whose name was Carrie, if she remembered correctly, strongly resembled her mother. It was like turning back the clock and seeing Catherine as the young college student who had loved and trusted Greg Bennett.

Shirley pinched her lips, disliking Greg Bennett more than ever. She wasn't one to suffer fools gladly.

"Greg Bennett needs a lot of help," she said, disheartened that their angelic talents were being wasted on a man who would neither acknowledge nor appreciate their endeavors.

Shirley figured that if the three of them stood directly in front of him in a full display of God's glory, Greg would turn around and head in the opposite direction.

"I bet Catherine didn't think so at the time, but the fact that Greg Bennett walked out on her was probably the best thing that could've happened. He's been a rotten husband to all three of his wives." Goodness shook her head in disgust. Apparently, she, too, was having difficulty finding him worthy of their assistance.

"What I don't understand," Mercy said, her expression thoughtful, "is why Gabriel would assign us someone who's so..." She floundered.

Goodness finished the sentence for her. "Impossible," she said. "Greg Bennett's *impossible*. And he doesn't care about God."

"But as we've discussed before, God cares about him, and so does Gabriel. Greg Bennett is the reason we're here," Shirley said. "The reason we had an opportunity to return to earth. It's our duty to make sure this is a Christmas he'll remember."

Both Goodness and Mercy stepped aside as Catherine and her daughter walked out of the restaurant, laughing and talking animatedly.

"You're right," Goodness agreed once mother and daughter had passed. "I don't like Greg Bennett any more than either of you, but God loves him." She began to say something else, then stopped abruptly. Her deep blue eyes grew huge. "Oh—look at that!"

"At what?" Shirley demanded.

"You'll never guess who's here," Goodness said excitedly. "Right now!"

Shirley whirled about, almost afraid to look. It couldn't be—but she knew it had to be. "Greg Bennett."

"We've got to *do* something," Mercy insisted. "Think, everyone. We can't let an opportunity like this pass."

"No...no!" Shirley cried, but Goodness and Mercy were already moving toward a table covered with steaming cooked crabs. "Not the crabs," but it was too late.

These Friday luncheon dates with her daughter were a delightful part of Catherine Thorpe's week. The hour with Carrie always went by in a flash. Meeting her daughter gave her an excuse to linger in the downtown area, as well. San Francisco in December was a sight to behold, and she planned to finish up her afternoon with some holiday shopping. She loved spoiling her grandson, and with another grandchild due in April, her world was full.

"I'll see you and Dad on Sunday, then," Carrie said as they strolled toward her office building.

"Bring Jason with you," Catherine urged. She

knew her daughter well enough to recognize that her current boyfriend was someone special.

"Mother," Carrie chided, "I don't—"

She was interrupted by a terrible clang. For no apparent reason, a table full of freshly cooked crabs toppled over, scattering them in every direction. Most of the contents slid across the pavement toward a strikingly attractive older man who leaped out of the way with enviable dexterity.

Catherine recognized Greg instantly, but she soon discovered that his gaze was focused on Carrie. He frowned, as if confused.

"Catherine?"

Carrie turned toward her mother and Greg's gaze followed. Catherine looked him full in the face, was looking at him for the first time in thirty-five years. Her lungs felt frozen and for a moment she couldn't breathe.

So this was Greg.

During the past decades Catherine had sometimes wondered how she'd react if she ever saw him again. Now she knew. Her mouth went dry, and the remembered pain of what he'd done made it difficult to swallow.

"Mom?"

Carrie's voice sounded as if it was coming from a great distance.

Catherine had to make a concerted effort to pull her attention back to her daughter.

"You look like you've seen a ghost," Carrie said worriedly.

"I'm fine," Catherine assured her daughter, but in fact, she *was* seeing a ghost. The ghost of a man who had destroyed her ability to love and trust. Time had dulled her bitterness toward Greg Bennett, had changed her feelings, but even all these years couldn't minimize the shock of seeing him so unexpectedly.

Before she could decide if she should approach Greg or ignore him, he took a step toward her, then hesitated. Catherine remained still. He slowly came closer until they stood face-to-face.

A flurry of activity went on about them as several people scurried to pick up the spilled crabs, but Catherine barely noticed.

"Catherine." Greg's voice was low, a little shaky.

"You know my mother?" Carrie asked, taking Catherine's arm protectively.

"Greg's an old friend," Catherine explained when it became apparent that Greg wasn't answering. She saw the way he stared at her daughter, and then she understood why. "Greg, this is my twenty-five-year-old daughter, Carrie Thorpe."

He picked up her message quickly. This wasn't his child, his daughter, and to his credit his recovery was smooth. "You're just as beautiful as your mother. When I first saw you I thought you *were* your mother."

Carrie blushed at the praise. "People tell me that

all the time." She suddenly glanced at her watch. "Oh, no. I hope you'll forgive me, but I have to rush back to work."

"Of course," Greg said as Carrie turned away.

"Goodbye, darling," Catherine called after her. "We'll see you and Jason Sunday for dinner."

When she was gone, Catherine looked at Greg. She'd always known this might happen, that she'd encounter Greg again, but now that she had, she wasn't sure what to do or what to say.

Greg seemed equally flustered. "It's been…a lot of years."

She gave a quick nod.

"Would you care to sit down?" he asked, then offered her a shaky smile. "Frankly, my knees feel like they're about to give out on me."

Catherine didn't feel much steadier herself. "That sounds like a good idea."

Greg led her to a sidewalk café, and when the waiter appeared, he ordered coffee for both of them. Although she normally drank her coffee black, Catherine added sugar to help her recover from the shock.

"Does Carrie have any older siblings?" Greg asked after a moment of stilted silence.

"A brother… I…had a boy seven months after you left," she said.

"You kept the baby?"

"Yes."

"You raised him?"

"Yes."

"Alone?"

She merely nodded this time, her throat thickening with the memory of the hardships she'd endured in those early years—the long hours, the hard work, the sleepless nights. "I...married when Edward was eight," she managed after a while, "and a year later Larry adopted him."

"So I have a son."

"No," Catherine told him, but without malice. "You are the biological father of a child. A wonderful young man who matured without the opportunity of ever knowing you. Without your ever knowing him."

Greg stared down at his coffee. "I was young. Stupid."

"Afraid," Catherine added softly. "We both were."

"But you weren't the one who ran away."

Catherine's laugh was wry. "I couldn't. I was the one carrying the baby."

Greg briefly closed his eyes. "I regret what I did, Catherine. I wanted to know what happened, but was afraid to find out."

"I know."

He looked at her then, as if he found it difficult to believe what she was saying.

Catherine glanced away. "It happened a very long time ago."

"I'm so sorry." He choked out the words, his voice raw with emotion.

"Don't say it," she whispered.

His face revealed his doubt, his confusion.

"You don't need to apologize, Greg. I forgave you years ago. You didn't realize it at the time and neither did I, but you gave me a beautiful gift in Edward. He was a wonderful child and a joy to my parents, who helped me raise him those first few years."

"You moved back home?"

"Until the baby was born. Then Mom watched him for me during the day while I finished college."

"It must have been difficult for you."

"It was." Catherine wasn't going to minimize the sacrifices demanded of her as a single mother. Those years had been bleak.

"Edward," Greg said. "After your father."

Catherine nodded, surprised he'd remembered her father's name.

"How could you forgive me?" Greg asked, sounding almost angry that she didn't harbor some deep resentment toward him. It was as if he expected her to punish him, to mete out her own form of justice right then and there.

"I had to forgive you, Greg, before I could get on with my life. After a while, the bitterness was more than I could endure. I had to leave it behind, and once I did, I discovered a true freedom. Soon afterward, I met Larry. We've been married for twenty-seven years now.''

''But I don't deserve your forgiveness.''

''That's not for me to say. But don't think forgiving you was easy, because it wasn't. When I first heard you'd left, I refused to accept it. I read your letter over and over—even though I couldn't take it in. I was convinced you'd be back. All you needed was time to sort everything out. I told myself you'd return to me and everything would be all right...but I had a rude awakening.''

''I...wasn't ready to be a father. I guess I never was.''

Catherine wondered if she'd misunderstood him. ''You mean to say you never had children?''

''None,'' he said. ''Three wives, but not one of them was interested in a family. For that matter, neither was I.'' He hesitated and his gaze skirted hers. ''I was a selfish bastard when I left you. Unfortunately that hasn't changed.''

She couldn't confirm or deny his words, for she no longer knew him.

''Would you mind telling me about Edward?'' he asked.

Catherine leaned back and sipped her coffee. ''In many ways he's very like you. The physical resemblance is there, anyway.''

Greg looked up and smiled faintly.

''He's six-two and muscular.''

"How old? Thirty-four?"

"Thirty-five," she told him. "His birthday was last month on the twenty-ninth."

"Is he married?"

"Yes, and he has a son himself and another baby on the way. Next spring."

Greg's smile grew wider.

"He's a doctor."

"Really?" Greg seemed to have trouble believing it.

"My husband is, too." Perhaps it was time to remind Greg who Edward's father was. "Larry raised Edward, helped make him the kind of man he is. Larry's his father."

Greg shook his head. "I wouldn't interfere in his life."

It took a moment for his words to sink in—and then it occurred to her what he'd meant. "Are you asking to meet Edward?"

Greg didn't respond for a long time. His face pale and intent, he finally said, "Yes. Could I?"

Four

Matthias Jamison enjoyed puttering around in his greenhouse before breakfast. The mornings—that was when he missed Mary the most. She'd been gone fifteen years now, and not a day passed that he didn't think about the woman he'd loved for more than thirty years. Some men he'd known were quick to remarry after losing their wives. Not him. Mary had been the only woman for him, and no one else would ever fill the void left by her death.

The sunrise over the Cascade Mountains was glorious, the light creeping up over the horizon, then spilling across his western-Washington vineyard like the promise it was. The morning sun was a reassurance, the pledge of another day, another opportunity. Mary had been the one to teach him that, but he'd never fully appreciated her enthusiasm for mornings until it was too late. He wished he'd shared more sunrises with his beloved wife.

Their only grandson now suffered from the same rare form of leukemia that had claimed her prematurely. It looked as if Tanner, too, would die. Matthias's jaw tensed and he closed his eyes. How could a loving God let an innocent child suffer like this?

What made an untenable situation even worse was the fact that his daughter bore the burden alone. Her ex had done nothing for her or the boy, making Matthias feel doubly responsible, but beyond phone calls and the occasional visit, there was little he could do to help her from where he lived.

The phone rang and Matthias hurried back to the house, hoping for good news. "Hello," he answered in his usual gruff voice.

"It's Harry."

A longtime friend and vineyard owner from the Napa Valley. "A little early for you to be phoning, don't you think?" Matthias couldn't prevent his disappointment from showing. He'd been hoping it was his daughter, Gloria, on the phone. He sighed heavily. It damn near killed Matthias that he was as powerless to help the boy as he'd been with Mary.

"I've got news that'll cheer you right up," Harry said.

"I could use some good news."

"It's about Greg Bennett."

Matthias stiffened at the sound of the name. He hated Greg Bennett with an intensity that had grown through the years. Bennett owed him. The success of the winery was largely due to Matthias's guiding hand. If it hadn't been for him, especially in those

early years, Greg would have lost the vineyard ten
times over.

The younger of the two Bennett boys had shown a
talent for the business, but Matthias had been the one
to teach him about grapes, about wine making, about
operating an estate winery. Greg's father, John Bennett, had lived for the vineyard, to the point that it
had destroyed his marriage. But he'd been impatient
with the boy, an ineffective teacher.

A few years after Greg had joined Bennett Wines,
John had died, and Greg had taken over. From that
point on, Matthias had advised Greg, guided him and
helped him expand enough to buy out his brother's
share. Matthias had treated Greg as he would have
treated his own son, if he'd had one. He'd shared
everything with Greg Bennett, his skills and ideas, his
enthusiasm for viticulture and wine making, his
friendship. That was what made the betrayal so painful, so devastating. Mary's illness was an almost in-
tolerable blow, but Greg's refusal to help them—that
had been, in a way, an even greater blow.

Mary had loved Greg, too. Many nights she'd insisted Greg join them for dinner. She'd opened her
home and her heart to Greg, and when she needed
him, he'd said no. Neither bonds of family nor friendship, neither obligation nor gratitude, had influenced
his decision.

"What about Greg?" Matthias asked now.

"He was in San Francisco looking for a loan."

So Greg's vineyard had been hit by fan leaf disease. Matthias had suspected as much, but hadn't heard. "Did he get one?"

Harry paused for effect. "Not a dime."

"Good."

"I thought you'd like hearing that."

Matthias did, but not nearly as much as he'd hoped. All his energy was focused on doing what he could to help his daughter and grandson. For fifteen years his hatred of Greg Bennett had simmered, until it'd burned a hole straight through his heart. He couldn't forgive or forget, but his hatred no longer dominated every waking moment.

"You always said time wounds all heels."

Matthias grinned. Actually, Mary had been the one to say that.

"He's going to lose everything."

"It's what he deserves," Matthias said without emotion. The younger man had laid the foundation of his own troubles. If anything, Matthias was grateful he'd lived long enough to witness Bennett's downfall.

"I bet you think he should rot in hell," Harry said, and when Matthias didn't comment, his friend spoke again. "Hey, I hate the guy, too. Everyone does— although not as much as you do." He chuckled. "Well, I better get back to my morning coffee."

"Thanks for the call."

"Talk to you later," Harry said. A moment later, the line was disconnected.

Matthias appreciated knowing of Greg's financial problems. Fan leaf, a virus, had indiscriminately infected a number of vineyards in both the Sonoma and Napa valleys. Owners had been forced to tear out formerly productive vines and start anew, a prospect that was both time-consuming and expensive. Many of the small and medium-sized wineries in the two valleys were in danger of going under, Greg's included.

Mostly retired, Matthias needed something to occupy his time. In recent years he'd been working with local vineyard owners who were trying to grow vines resistant to the fan leaf virus before it had the same devastating results in Washington as in California.

Standing next to the phone, Matthias realized he should be dancing at the news about the disaster at Bennett Wines. A year ago, even six months ago, he would have been thrilled at the thought of Greg's troubles. Revenge was said to be a dish best eaten cold, and he'd certainly waited long enough to have it served to him. But he experienced damn little of the pleasure he'd anticipated. He'd wanted Greg to suffer the same agony that had tormented him as he stood by his wife's bedside.

The vineyard was everything to Greg, just as Matthias's only grandchild had become everything to him. And this time, they were both going to lose what they loved most.

*   *   *

"That is so sad," Mercy said, sitting on the edge of the counter in Matthias's kitchen. "Just look at him."

"He's worried sick about his grandson."

"What's going to happen to the boy?" Both Goodness and Mercy turned to Shirley.

"Do I look like I have a crystal ball?" Shirley asked irritably.

"I don't know about you two—" Goodness reclined on the long counter "—but I was hoping for something a little less stressful during this visit to earth. We're assigned to a guy who's a real jerk. Someone who couldn't care less about anyone except himself."

"Yeah, but we're here on earth, aren't we?"

"Well, yes, but—"

"I agree with you," Shirley said, cutting in while the opportunity presented itself, "but we *can* help."

"Where's the fun? We got a human with his head so far up his—"

"Mercy!"

"A self-centered human," she revised. "You know, I think I'd feel better if Catherine had torn him to shreds. She should never have forgiven him."

"Mercy! Just listen to yourself."

"Right, right," she muttered, but Shirley could see that Greg was taking a toll on her friend's compassion.

"He's got too many problems for us to deal with," Goodness complained.

Shirley wasn't accustomed to such a defeatist attitude. "There's always his brother."

"What's this about a brother?" Goodness asked, suddenly attentive.

"Don't you remember?" Shirley did a double take. At their blank stares she sighed and reminded them. "Phil. You remember reading about Philip Bennett, don't you? He's a big muck-a-muck with Pacific Union Bank. Greg considered going to him for a loan, but couldn't bring himself to do it."

"Why not?"

Shirley sighed again. It would help considerably if Goodness and Mercy had finished their research.

"Refresh my memory, would you?" Goodness asked.

Shirley felt the burden of responsibility. "You didn't read the whole file, did you?" she asked wearily.

"Ah...no."

"That's what I thought." It would do no good to lecture them now. "Greg's mother was dying while he was in the middle of his second divorce."

"I remember reading about Bobbi," Mercy said triumphantly. "His second trophy wife."

"His second attempt to find another Catherine, you mean," Goodness muttered.

"Yeah, yeah. What does Bobbi and their divorce have to do with Greg's mother?" Mercy asked. Both angels were lying on their stomachs now, chins propped on their hands.

"You didn't finish reading the file, either?" Shirley was dismayed.

Anything that was going to get accomplished on this mission would obviously be up to her.

"It was too depressing."

"I don't have the patience to cope with men like him," Goodness said.

"Go on about his mother," Mercy urged, motioning with her hand for Shirley to continue.

"Greg hid as much of his wealth as he could from Bobbi, mostly in stocks and bonds. Otherwise she'd want her share in a divorce settlement."

"Were they married long enough for her to get much?"

Like most angelic beings, neither Goodness nor Mercy fully understood the way such matters were handled on earth. "Didn't matter," Shirley said. "She had a good attorney."

"Oh." Apparently Goodness and Mercy were knowledgeable enough to know what that meant.

"Lydia Bennett was dying and asked to see Greg," Shirley continued. "Unfortunately her request came the morning of his settlement hearing. Greg chose to go to court. I'm sure that if he'd known his mother would die before he got to the hospital, he would've canceled the court date."

"Oh, my," Goodness whispered.

"Phil never forgave him?"

"Never. They haven't spoken in ten years."

Goodness sat up and looked around. "I don't know if I can take much more of this. You two do what you want, but I need a break."

"Where are you going?" Shirley demanded. If her fellow angel got into any mischief, *she'd* be the one held accountable. As usual.

"Outside," Goodness called over her shoulder.

Without a word, Mercy followed Goodness.

"Mercy!" Shirley shouted.

Flustered now, she raced after the pair and came to an abrupt halt when she saw the hot-air balloons. Their huge parachutes with the bright rainbow-colored panels brightened the sky. There must have been a dozen balloons in the lower Kent Valley. She knew that conditions in the early-morning hours were often ideal for ballooning.

"Goodness! Mercy! Don't even think—" She was too late. Shirley caught sight of them as they hopped into a wicker carriage already filled to capacity. The ground crew was about to release the giant balloon from its tether line.

"Goodness!" Shirley called, exasperated beyond measure. "Mercy! Get out of there!"

Both pretended not to hear her. Shirley had to be careful. It wasn't uncommon for humans, especially young ones between the ages of one and five, to hear angels speak. Some older people possessed the ability, too. Inside the basket was an eighty-year-old grandmother who was taking the flight as a birthday gift from her grandchildren.

"For the love of heaven, will you two kindly—" Shirley froze, certain she was seeing things. The hot-air balloon had risen only about six feet off the ground, where it remained, hovering, even though the ropes that had bound the craft to earth had been set free.

"What's happening?" the old woman called to the ground crew, who'd stepped aside, obviously waiting for the balloon to glide upward. "Shouldn't we be going up?"

Shirley groaned when she saw the problem. Just as she'd ordered, Goodness and Mercy had indeed left the wicker basket, but had taken positions outside it, securing the dangling tether lines to the ground.

"Let go," Shirley yelled.

"Are you sure that's what you really want us to do?" Goodness asked.

Without waiting for a response, both Goodness and Mercy released their tether lines at the same time. The balloon shot into the sky like a rocket. A few seconds later, its speed became more sedate.

"Wow!" Shirley heard the grandmother shout, holding on to her protective helmet with one hand and gripping the basket with the other. "Can we do that again?"

Goodness stood next to Shirley, looking extremely pleased with herself.

''That felt wonderful.''

''You've risked the entire mission,'' Shirley said coldly. ''Gabriel is sure to hear about this.''

''Look at this,'' Mercy called as she joined them. She held a bottle of sparkling wine in one hand and dangled a trio of champagne flutes in the other.

''Where'd you get that?'' Shirley asked.

''They fell from the sky.'' She grinned broadly as she said it.

''Come on, Shirl,'' Goodness cajoled, ''humans aren't the only ones who enjoy a glass of bubbly now and then.''

Five

Greg had barely slept or eaten in five days. He hadn't recognized the gaunt beleaguered man who'd stared back at him in the bathroom mirror that morning. For a long time he'd studied his reflection, shocked into numbness. Anyone seeing him would assume his condition was due to either the stress of his vineyard being wiped out or the failure of his third marriage. Neither was true.

He had a son. Catherine had given birth to a boy, raised that child, loved him, guided him into adulthood. Now this child, the son Greg had rejected, was a doctor. His son was a father himself, which made Greg a grandfather. A grandfather! That knowledge was heady stuff for a man who'd never...never been a real father and never would be. When he'd abandoned Catherine and the child, Greg had assumed there'd be plenty of time for a wife and family. He hadn't realized back then that this child of Catherine's was his only chance. In his cowardice he'd thrown away the very life he'd always expected to have.

The first emotion he'd felt when Catherine told him

about Edward had been undiluted joy. He had no right
to feel anything—he knew that without her having to
say it—but it'd been impossible to hide his reaction.
Catherine always did possess the uncanny ability to
see through him. It was one reason he hadn't been
able to face her after she'd told him about the pregnancy. Evading responsibility, he'd run and hadn't
looked back—but he'd been looking back plenty
these past five days. Every waking minute, to be precise.

Greg wouldn't have blamed Catherine if she'd
ranted at him, called him every ugly name her vocab-
ulary would allow. But she hadn't. Instead, she'd offered him a gracious forgiveness, of which he felt
completely undeserving.

He could have accepted her anger far more easily
than her generosity of spirit. As unbelievable as it
seemed, *she* was the one who'd made excuses for the
shabby way he'd treated her.

All Greg could do was torment himself by thinking
of the opportunities he'd missed when he walked out
on Catherine. Since their meeting Friday afternoon,
the sick feeling in the pit of his stomach had refused
to go away. He didn't know what to do next, but one
thing was clear: he had to do *something*.

Catherine had said she'd get in touch with him
about his meeting Edward. He could tell she wasn't
keen on the idea; her pointed remark that Edward
already had a father had hit its mark. She'd said the

decision would come after she'd had a chance to talk it over with her husband, Larry, and with Edward himself. They'd parted then, with Catherine promising to call soon.

He hadn't heard from her since, and the waiting was killing him.

By five that evening Greg had lost patience and decided to call Catherine. He hurried into his office and reached for the telephone, intent on dialing directory assistance. As he lifted the receiver, a week's worth of mail slipped off his desk and onto the carpet.

With money pressures the way they were, Greg had been ignoring the mail, which consisted mainly of past-due notices and dunning letters from his attorneys. He stooped to pick up the envelopes, and that was when he saw it.

A letter addressed to him in Catherine's flowing penmanship. Thirty-five years, and he still recognized her beautiful handwriting.

Without conscious thought, he replaced the receiver. He studied the envelope carefully, noting the postmark. She'd mailed it the day after their meeting. He held it for a couple of minutes before he had the courage to open it.

The letter was brief.

Saturday, December 4
Dear Greg,
I'm sure you were as shocked to see me yester-

day as I was to see you. As I said, I always
thought we'd meet again one day, but I was still
unprepared for actually running into you.

I should have anticipated that you'd want to
meet the son you fathered. It was shortsighted of
me not to consider that before. I discussed it with
Larry. My husband is both wise and generous,
and he felt neither of us should be involved in
making such an important decision. He thought
I should leave it entirely up to Edward.

I was able to reach Edward yesterday evening.
It wasn't an easy conversation. He had a number
of questions—ones I'd been able to avoid until
now. I answered him truthfully; perhaps because
I did, he's decided against meeting you.

I'm sorry, Greg. I know this disappoints you.

Catherine

Greg read the letter a second time, then slumped in
his chair, eyes closed, while sharp pangs of disappointment stabbed him. It didn't escape his notice that
Catherine had used the same form of communication
he'd used when he deserted her. When he'd seen her
the previous week, he'd given her his business card
with his personal phone number. She could have put
him out of his agony days earlier; instead, she'd chosen to torment him. She'd probably derived a great
deal of satisfaction from turning him down, letting

him know he wasn't wanted. No doubt, she'd waited thirty-five years for the privilege.

In an outburst of anger he crumpled the letter and tossed it in the wastebasket. Still not satisfied, he swept his arm across the desktop, knocking everything onto the carpet. His chest heaving, he buried his face in both hands.

The Christmas spirit had infected Phil Bennett. He hummed along to ''Silent Night,'' which played on the bedroom radio, as he changed out of his business suit on Wednesday evening. Some people liked secular Christmas music the best, but Phil preferred the carols.

''You certainly seem to be in a good mood this evening,'' his wife remarked when he joined her in the kitchen for dinner. Sandy had grown a little thick through the waist over the past decade, but then, so had he. They'd been married for more than thirty years and raised three daughters and now they were both looking forward to retiring. The previous year, Phil and Sandy had purchased property in Arizona and planned to build in a retirement community, together with their best friends. It wouldn't be long now before the only real commuting he'd do would be on a par-three golf course.

''What makes you so happy?'' Sandy asked as she brought a platter of meat loaf to the small kitchen table. With the children grown and on their own, Phil and Sandy had taken to eating their meals in the kitchen, instead of the dining room.

"I don't know," Phil said, carrying over the tossed green salad. When she wasn't looking, he removed a sliced cucumber and munched on it.

"Well, then, I'm glad to see you've got the spirit of the season," Sandy said absently as she placed a bowl of steaming scalloped potatoes on a trivet.

"I do indeed," Phil murmured, even though it wasn't Christmas that had made him so cheerful. Actually, Christmas had very little to do with it, but he wasn't telling his wife that.

Once Sandy found out that his glee was entirely because of what he'd learned about his brother's financial woes, she was sure to lecture him. And Phil was in too fine a mood to be chastised.

Word had reached him that afternoon of Greg's numerous attempts to obtain financing for Bennett Wines. It did his heart good to learn that his ungrateful arrogant younger brother was about to receive the justice he so amply deserved.

"You're going to choir practice tonight, aren't you?" Sandy asked as she pulled out the chair across from him and sat down.

Caught up in his own thoughts, Phil didn't hear her right away. "Choir practice?" he repeated as he helped himself to a warm-from-the-oven biscuit.

"Phil!"

"Of course I'm going."

She relaxed. "Good. We need all the practice we can get."

Phil had recently joined the choir. It was his way of being part of the church community and contributing to the service.

So far, he knew only a few of the other choir members by name, but he'd know them all soon enough, especially now that they were meeting three nights a week to prepare for the Christmas cantata.

Unlike his brother, Phil was personable and generous—if he did say so himself. Plus, he had a reasonably pleasant singing voice. Greg didn't. Oh, his younger brother had certain talents, no question. He'd made Bennett Wines a respected label, well-known to wine cognoscenti. He had a single-minded focus that had led to his success. He could be charming when it was to his advantage.

And he was a ruthless bastard.

Phil had been waiting years for his brother to get what was coming to him. Years. The troubles currently plaguing California's wine industry had dominated the local news channels for weeks. Fan leaf virus was causing the ruin of many vineyards, and of course, Phil had wondered about Greg. But he hadn't heard anything definite until that very day. What he'd learned made him eager to sing.

After all these years, it was payback time. Greg had deserted a woman in need; Phil hadn't known Catherine well, but he'd liked her...and he'd heard rumors about a pregnancy. Then, perhaps worst of all, Greg had ignored his own mother on her deathbed, and when Phil had confronted him, he hadn't shown any genuine remorse.

Naturally, because of his religious beliefs, Phil tried not to hate his brother. He was willing to admit, though, that he felt strongly antagonistic toward Greg, not to mention gleeful about his financial woes.

He hadn't missed the fact that the one place Greg hadn't come to apply for a loan was Pacific Union. A wise decision. Given the opportunity, Phil would have relished personally refusing his brother's application. More than that, he'd done everything he could to make sure Greg didn't obtain funding. Actually, he'd handled that situation in a pretty clever way. He'd sent word through the banking community that when an application came to them from Bennett Wines, no one was to accept it. He'd given the impression that he'd be the one helping his brother.

If Sandy learned about this, she'd be furious. She'd accuse him of sabotaging Greg's business, but that wasn't how Phil viewed it. All he'd done was make sure Greg didn't get anything he didn't deserve. It'd probably be the first time, too. From childhood on, Greg had been the favored son. His fascination with that damned vineyard had guaranteed his special position with their father. And perhaps because he was the youngest, Greg had been coddled by their mother. Even when she was dying, she'd made excuses for him. It was now ten years since they'd buried their mother, and every time Phil thought about the funeral, the fury he still felt toward his brother threatened to consume him.

The grief Greg had shown was as phoney as a three-dollar bill. If he'd cared even a little about their mother, he would have come to the hospital when she asked for him. They'd known her illness was terminal! Nothing could have been more important; nothing should have kept him away. When Phil found out that Greg had chosen to attend the settlement hearing on his divorce case instead, he'd completely lost his temper.

The two brothers had nearly come to blows at the wake. What irked Phil the most was the grieving-son act Greg had put on for family and friends.

Grieving? Yeah, right.

Phil had been appalled by the number of people who seemed to fall for Greg's act. Phil had been hurting, too, but he'd disciplined himself not to show his emotions. Grief was private, after all. He'd also grown accustomed to the reality of her death, because he'd been there. His mother's illness had lasted several months, and Phil had been the one to sit at her bedside, to read to her and comfort her.

Sure, his brother had come to visit on occasion, but he always had a convenient excuse for not staying long. In the beginning it was because he was harvesting the grapes. That was followed by the wine-production period, which he said demanded constant supervision. During the last months of their mother's life, Greg had been involved in his divorce, too. His *second* divorce.

As far as Phil was concerned, his brother's marital problems were exactly what he deserved. The first wife, who'd lasted ten years, was bad enough. The second one, who looked shockingly like the first, had stayed around three years, possibly four, he couldn't remember. Phil had heard that there was a third Mrs. Greg Bennett, and he couldn't help wondering if she'd go the way of her predecessors.

"Phil, hurry, or we're going to be late," Sandy called from the kitchen.

They'd finished dinner and washed their few dishes, and while Sandy was collecting the sheet music, Phil watched the last of the national news.

"I'm ready," he called back, turning off the TV. Preoccupied with thoughts of his brother, Phil hadn't heard a word of the newscast.

The church parking lot was only partially filled when they arrived. The choir director smiled in greeting, but didn't allow anyone to waste time. The Christmas cantata was only two weeks away, and there remained plenty of room for improvement.

The choir members gathered on the bleachers; as a tenor, Phil stood in the back row behind the women singing first soprano. It wasn't until they started the first song that he noticed the blonde standing directly in front of him. He'd never heard anyone with a more spectacular voice. It was hard to remember his own part. The woman's clear strong voice was so stunning he was completely distracted.

"I don't believe we've met," he said during the break.

She turned around and smiled. "We haven't."

"Phil Bennett," he said.

"I know."

"You do?"

"Oh, yes. I know quite a bit about you, Mr. Bennett."

This was something. Phil squared his shoulders a bit, feeling downright flattered by this lovely woman's interest.

The director was pleased with their performance and after an hour and a half, dismissed them for the night.

"We sounded quite good, didn't we?" Sandy said on the drive home.

"I thought so, too. By the way, who was the woman standing in front of me?"

"Mrs. Hansen?"

"No, the blonde."

His wife cast him a curious look. "There wasn't any blonde standing in front of you."

"Yes, there was. We spoke. You couldn't have missed her, Sandy. She had the most angelic voice. Really gifted."

Sandy laughed softly. "And what was her name?"

Phil hesitated, trying to remember. "I don't believe she gave it to me."

"I see." Although Sandy wasn't actually smiling, he heard the amusement in her voice.

"I'm telling you there was a blond woman standing in front of me, and she sang like no one I've ever heard."

"If you say so, darling."

Women! If Sandy hadn't seen the blonde for herself, Phil couldn't make her believe she'd been there. Next practice, he'd be sure to introduce the woman to his wife. Then he'd see what Sandy had to say.

Six

"Goodness!" Shirley waited until the church had emptied before chastising her fellow angel. She just didn't know how to handle Goodness and Mercy. Their antics were going to get them permanently expelled from earth. "You had to do it, didn't you?"

At least Goodness had the decency to look properly repentant. "You're right, I know you're right, but I couldn't stand the smug way Phil Bennett was acting. From the moment he heard about his brother's problems, he was beside himself with pleasure. All his talk about being a good Christian, too!"

"We aren't here to deal with Phil Bennett."

"But he's part and parcel of what's happening to Greg."

"Well, yes, and no…"

"I don't think we need to worry," Mercy told her. "If Gabriel's going to be upset with us, it'll be because of what happened with the hot-air balloon. Goodness singing in a church choir is minor compared to that."

Shirley had done her utmost to put the balloon episode out of her mind, and Mercy's reference did nothing to calm her already tattered nerves. "Please, don't remind me."

"If Gabriel didn't hear about *that,* then we don't need to—" Mercy stopped midsentence. A panic-stricken look came over her face, and she blinked several times before she said, "Oh…hello, Gabriel."

"Hello, Gabriel," Goodness repeated, wide-eyed and subservient.

"The Archangel Gabriel to you," their boss said sternly.

Feeling slightly light-headed, Shirley turned around and swallowed nervously. She opened her mouth to offer a multitude of excuses and saw that it would do no good. Their chances of putting something over on the archangel were virtually nil.

"I'm here for a progress report," he announced in the same controlled voice.

Goodness and Mercy both gazed pleadingly at Shirley, silently begging her to respond. She glared at them. When she tried to speak, her tongue seemed glued to the roof of her mouth.

"Well?" Gabriel muttered. "I'm waiting."

"Greg talked to Catherine and he knows he fathered a son," Shirley blurted out.

"Are you telling me that after thirty-five years, Greg just *happened* to stumble upon Catherine?" Gabriel demanded.

Shirley was never sure how much Gabriel knew of

their antics, but suspected he was aware of it all. The questions were most likely a test to see how much they'd learned....

All three nodded in unison.

The archangel's frown darkened. "Thanks to a tableful of spilled crab, as I understand it."

"Yes, but that was only a means—"

"To an end," Gabriel completed for Mercy.

"Yes, and it worked very nicely, in my humble opinion," Goodness said in a bold rush. "It seemed a shame for the two of them to be in the same place after all those years and not know it. Really, all I did was point Greg out to Catherine. It was up to her to ignore or confront him."

"Yes," Mercy agreed. "Greg never did appreciate Catherine's strength."

"In other words, you're telling me," Gabriel said thoughtfully, "that Catherine chose to face him?"

Again all three nodded as one.

Gabriel's smile seemed involuntary. "The truth is, Catherine has Greg to thank for that inner strength. She gained it when he deserted her."

"They might never have met again if it hadn't been for those spilled crabs." Goodness made her foolishness sound like an act of genius.

Gabriel didn't look pleased—nor should he, Shirley reasoned. But that one antic *had* worked beautifully. She'd admit it now, even though she hadn't approved at the time.

"Do you have anything else to report?" Gabriel asked.

The three glanced at one another and shrugged.

"We've been to visit Matthias in the Seattle area," Mercy told him in an offhand manner meant to suggest that Gabriel probably already knew about it. "He still hates Greg, but he's more concerned about his grandson's condition just now."

"Ah, yes," Gabriel said, frowning again. "I've heard something about that. Cancer, is it?"

Shirley nodded. "The same form of leukemia that killed the boy's grandmother." Then, because she wanted to impress upon the archangel that their time on earth had been well spent, she said, "We've been to see Greg's brother, as well. Phil Bennett. You remember him, don't you?"

"Of course," Gabriel assured them. "I didn't realize Goodness enjoyed singing in choirs as much as she does. I'm sure she'll volunteer to be part of the heavenly host next year—is that correct?"

"Ah..." Goodness waited desperately for Shirley to rescue her, but Shirley was in no mood to offer assistance. She might have leaped in to save her friend, if not for that escapade with the hot-air balloon. She felt mortified every time she thought about it. True, the sparkling wine had gone a long way toward tempering her anger, but...

"I'll be happy to serve wherever assigned," Goodness stated with a woeful look in Shirley's direction.

Gabriel arched his brows as if to say her willingness surprised him. "I find your attitude a refreshing change from when we last spoke."

"Singing with the heavenly host isn't my favorite Christmas duty," Goodness was quick to add, "but I'll serve wherever you feel I'd do best."

Once again Gabriel's expression implied that he was having trouble believing her. "Anything else you'd like to report?" he finally asked.

"Not a thing," Shirley said, eager for him to be on his way.

"None."

"Nothing I can think of."

He stared at the three of them. "All right, then, carry on. Just remember there are less than three weeks until Christmas."

"Oh, yes," they said in unison. They'd made a lucky escape, Shirley felt. Gabriel hadn't even mentioned the hot-air balloon.

"It was very good of you to check up on us," Goodness said.

That was overdoing it, in Shirley's opinion. She resisted the urge to step on the other angel's foot.

"Oh, yes," Mercy chimed in. "Stop by again any time." For good measure, she added a small wave.

Shirley sent both Goodness and Mercy looks potent enough to perm their hair.

Gabriel turned away, then abruptly turned back. "I had no idea you three enjoyed wine."

Not one of them uttered a word. Shirley swallowed hard, certain they were going to be plucking harp strings on some cloud for the remainder of their careers.

"I don't suppose you happened to notice the label, did you?" he asked.

No one answered.

"That's what I thought," Gabriel said. "It was the Bennett label. Greg Bennett is a talented wine maker. It would be a pity for him to go out of business, don't you think?" Not giving them the opportunity to respond, Gabriel whisked back to the realms of glory.

Greg Bennett had an aversion to the antiseptic smell that permeated hospitals. It nearly overpowered him the minute he walked through the large glass doors of San Francisco General. His dislike of hospitals was linked to his mother's long stay before her death, he supposed. That, and his own revulsion to needles and blood.

He paused at the information center.

"Can I help you?" a much-too-perky candy striper asked him.

"Where might I find Dr. Edward Thorpe?"

"Oh, you're here about the article. That's wonderful!"

Article? What article? Greg hadn't a clue, but he played along as if he did. His son had decided he didn't want to meet him, and that was his choice, but

Greg wanted to see Edward. *Needed* to see him. He wasn't going to make an issue of it, wasn't going to announce who he was. He didn't plan to cause a scene or even call attention to himself. It was just that his curiosity had gotten the better of him....

Greg realized he'd given up his parental rights years ago, but he couldn't leave matters as they were. Not now that he knew Catherine had borne the child.

Catherine had mentioned the physical resemblance between them, and Greg felt an urge to simply see his son. He doubted they'd exchange a word. Without ever knowing him, without *wanting* to know him, Edward had rejected Greg.

Like father, like son.

"Take the elevator to the fifth floor." The young woman at the information desk pointed toward the row of elevators on the opposite side of the lobby. "Tell the nurse at the desk that you're here for the blood test."

"Ah." Greg hesitated. Did she say *blood?* He was most definitely not interested in anything to do with blood.

"I think it's wonderful of you," she added with a sweetness that made him want to cringe.

Greg didn't feel wonderful. Furthermore, he had no intention of giving anyone a drop of his blood. Not without one hell of a fight first.

"Dr. Edward Thorpe—you're sure he's there?"

"He's on the fifth floor," the woman assured him. "Just ask for him at the nurses' station."

"Thank you," he said, turning toward the bank of elevators.

"No, thank *you*," she called after him.

Greg got off the elevator at the fifth floor and to his surprise walked into a corridor filled with people. As instructed, he headed for the nurses' station, but before he could say a word, he was handed a clipboard.

"Complete the form, sign the bottom of the page and bring this back to me when you're finished."

Greg stared at the woman. "What's it for?"

"We need you to fill out the questionnaire and sign the release if we're going to take your blood." Unlike the perky candy striper, this one looked harassed and overworked.

"I realize that, but—"

"Just read the form. If you have any questions after that, I'll be happy to answer them."

That sounded fair enough. Greg joined the others, sat down and read the page. It was exactly what the nurse had said. Basically, San Francisco General was requesting permission to draw blood. Not that he'd give it. Not in this lifetime.

As soon as he finished reading the form, he knew it was time to leave. He was about to pick himself up and discreetly disappear when a physician entered the room.

Conversation stopped as the man stood before the group and started to speak. Greg glanced up and froze. It was Edward. He recognized him immediately, long before he looked at the identification badge that hung around his neck.

"Has everyone finished signing the waiver?" Dr. Thorpe asked. "If you've decided this isn't something that interests you, you can leave now. We appreciate your time. For those of you who wish to continue, we promise to make this as quick and painless as possible. Before you know it, you'll be on your way."

Three or four people left the room.

Greg could follow them or proceed with this. Swallowing his natural aversion, he quickly signed his name. Okay, so he had to give a little of his blood. No big deal. He'd give a lot more if it meant he could spend a few minutes getting to know his son.

Catherine was right about one thing. Edward was tall and distinguished-looking, but as far as family resemblance went, Greg didn't see it. Still, he couldn't stop staring. This was *his* son. Edward looked good. Damn good. One glance had told Greg that his son was everything he wasn't. Dedicated. Compassionate. Smart.

"I'll need that," the nurse said as Greg shuffled past.

He gave her the clipboard and walked down the corridor, along with the others.

"Before we go any further," Edward said, "I want

to personally thank each of you for your generous response to the recent newspaper article. We didn't have this many volunteers in the entire month of November. I'd like to think the Christmas spirit has touched us all. Does anyone have any questions?''

A man with prematurely white hair raised his hand. ''What will happen if we're a match?''

While Edward talked about obscure-sounding medical procedures, Greg leaned toward the woman standing ahead of him. ''A match for what?''

''Bone marrow,'' she muttered out of the corner of her mouth, then turned to eye him. ''Are you sure you're supposed to be here?''

If ever a question needed answering, this was it.

''No,'' he said more to himself than to her. He wasn't sure of anything. Curiosity had brought him to the hospital. A curiosity so deep it had consumed him for days. After thirty-five years of not knowing, not caring, he now felt an overwhelming desire to see his son.

''Who'd like to go first?''

Before Greg could stop himself, he shot his hand into the air.

''Great. Follow me.'' Greg stepped out of the line and followed his son down the corridor to a cubicle.

''The nurse will be right in to draw blood.''

''Aren't you going to take it yourself?'' Greg asked. Already he could feel his panic level rise.

Edward shrugged lightly. "Well...the nurse usually does this."

"I'd prefer if you did it yourself. In fact, I insist on it."

Surprise showing in his eyes, Edward turned to face him. It seemed he was about to refuse, but for reasons Greg wouldn't question, silently led him to a chair and instructed him to sit down.

Greg sat, unbuttoned his shirtsleeve and rolled it up.

"Do I know you?" Edward asked, studying him carefully.

"No," Greg responded. "Do I remind you of anyone?" He was well aware that this was an unfair question.

"No, but I thought you might be a friend of my father's, Dr. Larry Thorpe."

"No, I've never met him."

Edward took a short piece of what looked like rubber tubing and tied it around Greg's upper arm. Next he gingerly tested the skin. "Nice blood vessels. We shouldn't have any problem."

"Good." Greg's mouth went dry at the sight of the needle, and closing his eyes, he looked away. This was even worse than the last time he'd had blood tests. He felt the needle against his skin and braced himself for the small prick of pain. As a kid he'd fainted in the doctor's office every time he received a shot or had blood drawn; he wasn't keen to relive the experience. That was years ago, but even now, as an adult, he generally avoided annual checkups if he could and— The needle was the last thing he noticed until he heard Edward's voice, which seemed to boom at him like a foghorn.

"Are you awake?"

Greg blinked and realized he was lying on the floor. Edward knelt beside him.

Their eyes met, and embarrassed, Greg glanced away. "What happened?" he asked, still in a daze.

"You passed out."

"I did?" Abruptly Greg sat upright. He would have fled, but the room had started to swim in the most disturbing fashion.

"Take it slowly," Edward advised, then helped him stand up. "I've asked one of the nurses to take your blood pressure. Tell me, when was the last time you had anything to eat?"

"I'm fine. I had breakfast this morning." It was a lie. He wasn't fine and he hadn't eaten breakfast. "I just don't happen to like needles."

"Then it's a brave thing you did, coming in here like this."

"Brave?" Greg repeated with a short laugh. "I'm the biggest coward who ever lived."

Seven

On Monday morning Greg recognized that he had no other options left to him. It wouldn't be easy to apply for a loan at Pacific Union Bank, but he had nowhere else to go. He'd never been a person to beg. Never *needed* to beg until now, but if begging would help him hold on to Bennett Wines, he'd do that and more.

The worst of it was that he'd have to go begging to his own brother. Phil, who'd like nothing better than to call him a failure. He wouldn't be far from wrong; Greg *felt* like a failure.

Despite his mood, Greg prepared carefully for the interview, wearing his best suit. He was about to head out the door when his phone rang. Caller ID told him it wasn't a creditor.

"Hello," he snapped.

"Hello, Greg."

It was Tess, his almost ex-wife. Ex-wife number three. "What's the matter? Are you after another pound of flesh?" he sneered. The last thing he needed right now was to deal with spoiled selfish Tess.

"I heard about your money problems."

"I'll bet you're gloating, too."

He heard her intake of breath. "I don't wish you ill, Greg."

He didn't believe her for a moment. "What do you want?" He was facing an unpleasant task that demanded all his attention, and he didn't want to be waylaid by an even more unpleasant one.

"I called because I didn't realize the extent of your money problems until now and, well...I'm sorry."

He said nothing.

"I wish you'd told me earlier. If I'd known, perhaps—"

"Would it have made any difference?" Their troubles had started long before the fan leaf virus had destroyed his vines. Long before he'd been confronted with one financial crisis after another. He knew when he and Tess got married that they were probably making a mistake. Still, that hadn't stopped him. He'd wanted her, and she'd wanted the prestige of being married to him. True, they looked good together, but at the moment it seemed that was *all* they'd had going for them.

He didn't like living alone, but he figured he'd get used to it eventually.

She didn't answer his probing question right away. "If I'd known about your troubles, I like to think it would have changed things."

All women preferred to believe the best about

themselves, he thought cynically. "Think what you like," he muttered.

"Oh, Greg, do you hate me that much?"

Her words caught him up short. "I don't hate you at all," he said, and realized it was true. He was sorry to see the marriage end, but he hadn't been surprised and, in fact, had anticipated their divorce long before Tess moved out.

"You don't?" She sounded surprised, but recovered quickly. "Good, because I was thinking we should both do away with these attorneys and settle matters on our own. I can't afford three-hundred dollars an hour, and neither can you."

Greg wasn't sure he should put too much faith in this sudden change of heart. "Do you mean it?"

"Of course I do."

"All right, name a date and a time, and I'll be there." Greg hated the eagerness that crept into his voice, but he wanted the attorneys out of these divorce proceedings as much as Tess did. Without them—stirring up animosities, asking for unreasonable concessions—he and Tess had a chance of making this separation amicable.

"How about next Tuesday night?" she suggested.

Greg noted the time and place and, with a farewell that verged on friendly, they ended the call.

Well, well. Life was full of surprises, and not all of them unpleasant.

The drive into the city, however, could only be

called unpleasant. Traffic was heavy and Greg soon lost his patience, particularly when it took him nearly an hour to find parking, and that wasn't even close to the financial district. The cost of parking in San Francisco should be illegal, he grumbled to himself. This was his third trip into the city within ten days; he hadn't been to San Francisco three times in the entire previous year. Greg preferred his role as lord of the manor—a role that was about to be permanently canceled if he couldn't secure a loan.

The sidewalks were crowded, since it was almost lunchtime. A brisk wind blew off the bay and he hunched his shoulders against it, ignoring the expensive-looking decorations on the bank buildings and the tasteful Christmas music floating out from well-appointed lobbies as doors were opened.

He sincerely hoped he wouldn't be forced to see Phil this early in the process, if at all. Knowing Phil as he did, Greg was keenly aware that his brother would take real pleasure in personally rejecting his application. Then again, he might exercise some modicum of mercy and leave it to someone else, a junior officer. But that wasn't something Greg needed to worry about just yet. Today was only the first step— meeting with a loan officer and completing the lengthy application. Once he'd finished the paperwork, he could leave. Walk out the doors of yet another bank, wait for yet another rejection.

He hated his own pessimistic attitude, but nothing

had happened in the past week to give him any hope. His brother hated him—it was that simple—and Phil wasn't the kind of man to put their argument behind him. If he hadn't forgiven Greg in ten years, he wasn't likely to do it now.

Phil had always been somewhat jealous of him, Greg knew, something he'd never really understood. Greg supposed his greatest sin was the fact that he'd been born last. That, and sharing a passion for wine making with his father. Despite what Phil believed, Greg had loved their mother. Her death, although expected, had hit him hard.

He'd had no way of knowing how critical her condition was. They'd spoken briefly the night before, and while she'd sounded weak, she'd encouraged him to take care of his own business, to keep his appointment at court. So he'd felt there was still plenty of time. She hadn't seemed that close to death.

His fight with Phil after the funeral had been the lowest point in his life. The truth was, Phil hadn't called him any name he hadn't called himself in the years since.

When Greg had finished with the loan application at Pacific Union, he walked back to the parking lot and paid the attendant what amounted to a ransom. But instead of heading for the St. Francis for a good stiff drink as was his custom, Greg drove to Viewcrest, the cemetery where his mother was buried.

He spent more than an hour wandering down long grassy rows in the biting wind before he located his mother's grave. He stood there, gazing down at the marker. *Lydia Smith Bennett, 1930-1989 Beloved Mother.* Phil had arranged for that stone. Phil had made all the arrangements.

This was Greg's first visit since they'd buried her. He shook his head, brushing away tears, over-whelmed by all the things he'd left unsaid. *I loved you, Mom. I did. I do. I'm sorry…*

Eventually he squatted down, touched his fingers to his lips and pressed them to the marble gravestone. A long moment passed before he stood up again, shoulders bent, head bowed, and silently walked away.

"Has anyone got a tissue?" Mercy wailed, and when no one responded, she threw herself against Goodness, wiping her face on her friend's soft sleeve.

"Would you kindly *stop?*"

But Goodness sounded suspiciously tearful. Shirley, too, was having a hard time holding back her emotions. Seeing Greg like this, broken and defeated, was painful. She barely recognized him anymore. She didn't know when it had happened or how, but she'd started to care about this man. Obviously Goodness and Mercy had also revised their feelings toward him.

"We've got to do something to help Greg!"

"We're trying," Shirley said.

"But he's in bad shape."

"I have a feeling it's going to get worse," Shirley whispered, fearing the future.

"Say it isn't so." Mercy wailed all the louder.

"His brother's going to reject the loan, isn't he?" Shirley couldn't imagine Phil making any other decision and said as much.

"Not if I have anything to say about it," Goodness cried. "I think it's time I got ready for choir practice again, don't you?"

"Goodness, no!"

"I don't care if Gabriel sends me back to singing with the heavenly host or even gatekeeping. Phil Bennett is about to get a piece of my mind."

"Goodness." Mercy gasped.

"What?"

"Goodness," Shirley began. "You—"

"I'm going, too." Mercy glanced at Shirley.

Shirley could see she had no choice. "Oh, all right, but we can't all three join the choir."

"Why not?" Mercy asked, rushing to catch up with Goodness.

Shirley shook her head in wonder, sure they'd be facing the wrath of Gabriel once again. She just hoped the sacrifice they were prepared to make on Greg Bennett's behalf would turn out to be worth it.

"Phil, I swear you haven't heard a word I've said all evening."

Phil lowered the evening newspaper and looked at his wife. "What gives you that impression?"

Sandy threw back her head with a frustrated groan and returned to the kitchen.

Reluctantly Phil followed her. He should have known better than to try bluffing his way out of this. After all these years of marriage, there wasn't much he could hide from Sandy. He *was* preoccupied, true. It had to do with his brother. His shiftless irresponsible no-good brother who'd once been everyone's golden boy. Well, not anymore.

"Greg was in the bank this afternoon," Phil told Sandy in a nonchalant voice, pouring himself a cup of coffee.

He had Sandy's full attention now. "Did you talk to him?" She knew as well as he did that they hadn't spoken since their mother's funeral.

"No-o-o." He shrugged and tried to look regretful. "Dave Hilaire was the one who dealt with him."

"Greg's applying for a loan?"

Phil replied with a somber nod, but he felt like jumping up and clicking his heels.

"I've been reading for weeks about the problems the wineries have been experiencing," Sandy said thoughtfully. "It must be terrible to have some virus wipe out generations of work. From what I read, some vineyards were more badly hurt than others."

"Greg's vineyard is one of the worst hit," Phil explained in the same grave voice.

"I wondered about Bennett Wines...."

"Me, too." He did his best to sound sympathetic.

Sandy studied him, her eyes narrowed, and Phil struggled to hide his true sentiments. This virus, or something like it, was exactly what he'd been waiting for. *Justice. Retribution. Revenge. Call it what you will.* Phil had suspected that sometime or other, Greg would come crawling to him, asking for help. He'd anticipated that day, longed for it.

"Are you going to be able to get him the loan?"

"I...I don't know," Phil hedged. He could hardly admit that he'd wear thong underwear in public before he'd sign off on the money Greg needed.

"But you'll do what you can?" Sandy gave him a hard look, and it was all he could do to meet her eyes.

"Of course," he said, sounding as sincere as he could.

She sighed, then walked over to him and kissed him on the cheek. "Good. I've always hoped you two would put aside your differences."

Phil hugged her rather than look her in the face. "I know."

"You're all Greg has in the way of close family."

True, but that hadn't made any difference to his brother, and Phil didn't see why it should to him. Greg would come to him when he needed help and only because he needed help. So, any apology, any effort toward reconciliation, was tainted as far as Phil was concerned. Not that he intended to forgive his brother or had any interest in reconciling with him. It was too late for that. A just God would surely understand that some things were unforgivable. Wouldn't He?

"Poor Greg," Sandy whispered.

Oh, yes, and Greg wouldn't know how truly poor he was until Phil had finished with him.

"No wonder you weren't listening earlier," Sandy said, freeing herself from his embrace. "You had other things on your mind."

"I'm sorry, honey."

"You *are* going to help him, right?" Sandy was obviously seeking reassurance.

He nodded, still without looking at her.

"Fine. You'll be busy with that, so let's skip the practice. I'll tell Evelyn we can't do it."

Evelyn was the choir director. "Can't do what?"

"Go caroling Christmas Eve."

"Just a minute," Phil said. "Why not? We don't have anything on the schedule, do we? None of the girls can come until Christmas morning."

"You're sure you still want to?" Sandy asked, sounding pleased.

"Very sure."

"You're just hoping to see that blonde again, aren't you?" she teased.

The blonde he'd spoken with earlier in the week hadn't shown up for practice the last two times, and

Phil was growing discouraged. She hadn't been a figment of his imagination, despite what Sandy claimed.

"Maybe I did just imagine her," he said to appease Sandy. "I have to keep you on your toes, don't I?"

"We're going to be singing at the hospital Christmas Eve. San Francisco General." Sandy eyed him as though expecting Phil to change his mind.

"That's all right." Not exactly his favorite place, but he could live with it.

Besides, singing carols for the sick was what Christmas was all about. This was the season of love and goodwill, and he had an abundant supply. Not for his brother, but that was Greg's own fault. "As a man sows, so shall he reap." That was somewhere in the Bible, and if anyone questioned his actions, Phil would happily quote it.

Oh, yes, his brother was getting exactly what he deserved.

Eight

Matthias stepped off the plane and walked through the long jetway to the terminal at San Francisco International Airport. He'd come to spend Christmas with his grandson, fearing it would be the boy's last.

He spotted his daughter in the crowd and rushed toward her. "Gloria," he whispered, hugging her close. She'd lost weight and looked pale and fragile. This was destroying her—to watch her son dying, one day at a time. Matthias remembered how emotionally drained he'd become when Mary had been so terribly ill. Gloria had suffered then, too—and now she had to go through all this grief and pain again.... How could she bear it?

"Oh, Daddy, I have wonderful news!" his daughter exclaimed. "A donor's been found."

The unexpected relief, the gratitude Matthias suddenly felt made him go weak. "Where?" he asked hoarsely. "Who is it?"

"I don't know his name. He's a stranger, someone who responded to the article in last week's newspaper about the need for volunteers. Dr. Thorpe says he's making the phone call this afternoon and the whole process should start before Christmas. Isn't that *wonderful?* Oh, Daddy, I can't tell you how happy I am!''

"It's the best Christmas gift anyone could have given me."

"Me, too." Gloria's eyes shone with unshed tears. "Dr. Thorpe says the match is an especially good one. He sounded really hopeful, Dad. He didn't come right out and tell me this was going to save Tanner's life, but it is, I know it is. My heart tells me everything's going to be all right now." No longer did she struggle to hold back the tears. They fell unrestrained down her cheeks.

"When can I see this grandson of mine?" Matthias asked, eager now to reach the hospital.

They chatted nonstop on the drive into the city. When they got to the hospital, they hurried to the eighth floor. Weak as he was, ten-year-old Tanner was sitting up in bed waiting for Matthias.

"Merry Christmas, Grandpa." His pale face was wreathed in an extra-wide grin, although his eyes were sunken and shadowed.

"Merry Christmas, Tanner." Matthias hugged his grandson, careful not to hurt the fragile little body. Seeing him like this was hard. So hard.

"Grandpa, are you crying?"

"It's only because I'm happy." Matthias glanced up and smiled apologetically at his daughter and the young nurse who stood beside her.

"Everything's going to be all right now," Gloria assured him again, and Matthias believed her. Everything *was* going to be better.

"Hello," Greg snapped into the small cellular phone. He'd never enjoyed talking on the telephone and was particularly annoyed by these newfangled cell things.

"Is this Greg Bennett?"

"Yes." Again his voice was as sharp and short-tempered as he could make it. He was walking between the rows of dead and dying grapevines, recognizing with final certainty that nothing was salvageable. No one could save what had taken fifty years to build.

"This is Dr. Edward Thorpe from San Francisco General."

Greg was so shocked he nearly dropped the phone. "Yes…Dr. Thorpe."

"I was wondering if you'd be willing to come back to the hospital later this afternoon?" His voice was pleasant, smooth, and if Greg wasn't mistaken, there was a hint of relief, too.

"I'll be there," Greg told him immediately.

"I realize it's short notice and this is the Christmas season, but—"

"I'll be there," Greg interrupted. "What time?"

"Is three o'clock convenient?"

"Sure." Then he couldn't resist asking, "Can you tell me what this is about?"

"I'd prefer we discuss it once you get here." He ended the conversation by giving Greg detailed instructions on where and how to reach him at the hospital.

"I'll see you at three," Greg said, then slipped the phone back into his shirt pocket. He drew in a deep breath, releasing it slowly.

Somehow, some way, Edward had discovered the truth about their relationship. Apparently his son had experienced a change of heart and decided to meet his biological father, after all.

Although Greg could offer no excuse for what he'd done to Catherine, he was grateful for Edward's decision. He did want Edward to know that he was proud to have fathered him, proud of the man he'd become. Greg could claim no credit; Edward owed him nothing. He only hoped that one day his son would be able to forgive him. He'd like a relationship with him, but wouldn't ask. That, like everything else, was up to Edward.

The drive into the city was becoming almost routine by now. Greg found he was nervous and at the same time excited. He parked where Edward had suggested and followed the directions he'd been given. Not until he was in the elevator did he realize the hospital's antiseptic smell hadn't overpowered him. That, he decided, was a good sign.

Edward was waiting when he arrived and personally escorted him into his office. Greg noted with
some satisfaction that Edward was as tidy and orga-
nized as he was himself. The physician's desktop held
a pen-and-pencil set, a clock and a computer monitor.
On the credenza behind him was a small collection
of framed photographs. He recognized Catherine in
one, beside a tall gray-haired man, obviously her husband.

"Your wife?" Greg asked, looking past him to the
gold-framed photograph of a younger woman.

Edward nodded.

"I've been married three times," Greg blurted out,
then wanted to kick himself.

His son had the good grace to ignore that comment.
"I suppose you've guessed why I asked you to stop
by the hospital."

Greg liked the fact that Edward was forthright
enough to get to the point immediately. "I have an
idea."

"Good," he said, and seemed to relax. "That being
the case, I'd like to introduce you to someone very
special."

Greg hesitated. "Now?" To his mind, there were
several things they should discuss before he met anyone important in Edward's life, but he was willing to
let his son chart their course.

"If you don't mind, that is?"

"All right." Greg was simply grateful for this unexpected opportunity. His miserable attempt to see Edward earlier in the week had failed and humiliated him. Thankfully, Edward hadn't seen fit to remind him of what had happened at their last meeting.

Edward led him to the elevators and together they rode silently up several floors. They stopped at what appeared to be a children's ward. Greg frowned. Without asking any questions, he followed Edward to a room at the end of the corridor.

"This is Tanner Westley," Edward whispered, nodding toward the sleeping youngster.

From the tubes and other medical equipment linked to the emaciated body, Greg could tell the boy was gravely ill.

"Should I know him?" Greg asked, also in a whisper.

Edward shook his head. "Let's return to my office and I'll explain the procedure."

Procedure? Greg wasn't sure he understood, but he accompanied Edward back to his office.

When they entered the room and resumed their seats, Edward said, "I can't tell you how delighted I was that you proved to be a match for Tanner."

"Match?"

"Bone-marrow match," he said, eyeing Greg closely. "I assumed you understood the reason for my call."

"No. No way." Before he knew it, Greg was on his feet, emphatically shaking his head. "You want me to be a bone-marrow donor? This is a joke, right? You saw for yourself what happens any time I have blood taken.''

''But you did come into the hospital for the test. Surely you realized—''

''There's no way in hell you're going to get me to agree to this!''

''Please, sit down.'' Edward motioned calmly to the chair.

He made an effort to fight back his disappointment. This meeting had nothing to do with Edward wanting to know his birth father—it was all about what he could do to help some *stranger*. Greg continued to shake his head. No amount of talk, even from his son, would convince him to let someone stick another needle in his arm. Or anyplace else, for that matter.

''Before you refuse, let me explain the procedure.''

''You have a snowball's chance in hell of talking me into this,'' Greg felt obliged to tell him. He sat down, crossing his arms defensively.

''Two weeks from now, Tanner will be placed in an aseptic room where all his bone-marrow cells, both the good ones and the bad ones, will be destroyed by high doses of chemicals and radiation. This is the only way we have of completely eradicating the malignant cells.''

''Doc, listen—''

''Let me finish, please, and if you still feel the same way after that, then…well, then we can talk.''

Greg groaned silently and saw that he had no choice but to listen. Once Edward was finished, he would make some excuse and leave by the fastest route possible.

"This will be a dangerous time for Tanner, when he's most susceptible to infection.

"On the day of the transplant, the bone marrow will be extracted from you and stored in a blood bag, then intravenously transfused into Tanner over the course of several hours." He paused and studied Greg, who sat quietly, without moving. "Do you want to ask me about the pain or how the marrow is extracted?"

"Not particularly." He didn't need to know, didn't care to know, seeing that it wasn't going to happen.

"Most people are curious about the pain, and rightly so. I won't deny that there is some discomfort involved in this process, but I like to tell my donors that it never hurts to save a life."

Apparently Edward hadn't heard him correctly the first time. Greg wasn't doing this. *Couldn't* do this.

"I want to schedule the procedure as quickly as possible. As you can see, Tanner's health is failing."

Greg stared at him, wondering why Edward refused to understand. "Don't schedule anything for me. You'll just have to find another donor."

Now it was Edward's turn to wear a shocked disbelieving look. "You really won't do it?"

"Not on your life."

"It isn't *my* life or *your* life you're sacrificing. It's that young boy's. He'll die without a bone-marrow transplant."

"You'll find another donor." Greg stood, desperate to escape.

"No, we won't." Edward stood, too. "Do you think just anyone can supply the bone marrow for Tanner? If that was the case, I'd give him my own— but it's not. There has to be a match. You're that match."

"Don't see how I can be," Greg said stubbornly. He wasn't any relation to the boy.

"Why did you sign the release and agree to have your blood tested if you weren't willing to be a donor?" Edward raised his voice.

Greg dared not tell him the truth, dared not announce the real reason he'd come to the hospital.

"Did you take a good look at Tanner?" Edward asked. "He's only ten. He could be your son or even mine, and he's only got a very small chance of living without your bone marrow."

"And *with* my marrow?" Greg couldn't believe he'd even asked.

"There's a much greater likelihood that he'll see another Christmas."

Greg slumped back in the chair and covered his eyes with the heels of his hands. He didn't know what to do.

* * *

"Is he going to do it?" Mercy cried, pacing the area directly behind Edward's desk. "I can't stand not knowing."

"Shush! I can't hear." Goodness waved a quieting arm at Mercy.

"Shirley, do *you* know?" Mercy asked.

Shirley shook her head.

"He's going to refuse?" Mercy collapsed against a bookcase. "Has the man no heart?"

"Would you kindly stop that noise?" Goodness warned a second time. "I can't hear a thing."

"They're arguing," Shirley said. "And poor Greg has no way of knowing—"

"That Tanner is Matthias's grandson?"

"No, not just that," Shirley said sadly. The irony here had God's fingerprints all over it.

"No?" Goodness paused to look in Shirley's direction, clearly puzzled.

"What Greg doesn't know," Shirley told her two friends, "is that the boy is more than Matthias's grandson. He's Greg's chance for redemption."

Nine

Phil and Sandy Bennett arrived five minutes late for choir practice. Weaving his way between choir members, Phil climbed into his position on the riser, frazzled and irritated with his wife. Sandy might not have intended to make him feel guilty about Greg—but somehow he did. Well, not guilty exactly. A little uncomfortable, perhaps.

It wasn't until he opened the sheet music and started singing along with the others that he heard her. The blonde who sang first soprano was back! Gradually the tension between his shoulder blades relaxed. He knew it; she hadn't been imaginary at all. He waited until the last notes had died down, then casually leaned forward to speak to her.

"Where have you been?" he asked her, unable to disguise his excitement. Before she could answer, he asked another question. "What's your name?" It would have helped if he'd had a name to give Sandy. She knew a lot more of the choir members than he did.

"I've been busy," she told him.

"You're a member of the choir, though, aren't you?"

"I'm here."

Her hair was so blond it was almost white, and her singing voice... Phil had never known anyone who could sing quite like this woman. Her voice had a power and beauty that was almost unearthly.

"I've got to introduce you to my wife," he said while they shuffled through their sheet music, preparing for the next carol.

"What about your brother?" she asked. "Don't you want to introduce me to him, too?"

The music started before Phil had a chance to recover. "You know my brother?" he asked as soon as the last notes had died away.

"Oh, yes. I know a lot about you both."

"Who are you?" He didn't like the turn their conversation was taking.

"A friend."

Phil was beginning to wonder about that.

"You have Greg's loan application on your desk, don't you?"

How she knew that, he wouldn't ask. He'd been reading it that very afternoon just before he'd left the office, but only one person in the entire loans department was aware of it. He narrowed his gaze and studied this woman, who seemed to know more about him than she should.

"You haven't forgiven him for what he did to your mother, have you?"

"Damn straight I haven't."

"Then it might surprise you to learn that he hasn't forgiven himself, either."

"Pigs will fly before I believe he has one iota of remorse."

Frieda Barney turned around and glared at Phil. Someone else indicated her displeasure with his talking by pressing her finger to her lips. From the opposite end of the riser he could feel his wife's look burn right through him.

The music started again and Phil did his best to remain focused on it. The warmth he'd felt toward the beautiful willowy blonde had evaporated. By some corrupt means, his brother had finagled this…this spy into the church choir one week before Christmas. Greg always had been a good manipulator.

"You haven't spoken to him in all these years." A second voice came from beside him. This woman was slightly taller than the other. A second blonde? And one who sang? That didn't make sense. He closed his eyes, then opened them again, thinking he was losing his mind.

"Who are you?" he demanded in an angry whisper.

"The more appropriate question would be who are *you*."

"I know who I am."

"Do you?" the second woman asked. "Do you really?"

"You've always thought of yourself as the good brother," the first soprano chided.

"The churchgoer."

"The choir member."

"Yet all the while you've been plotting your brother's downfall, relishing it. You can hardly wait to see him suffer."

Female voices were coming at him from every direction. Not one voice, not even two, but three distinct voices. He thought he'd go mad if he heard another word. "Would you kindly *shut up*."

The room abruptly went silent. Everyone turned to stare at him. "I'm sorry," Phil mumbled. He could feel the heat rush into his face as he returned his attention to his music. He didn't know what had come over him.

Evelyn, the choir director, looked at him sternly. "Is everything all right?"

"Yes, I'm sorry. It won't happen again."

The director asked the altos to go over a particularly tricky piece of music while the others waited. They'd just sung the first line when the blondes started in on him again. "It's the season of brotherly love," the one beside him said. "I'm beginning to wonder if you know what that means."

Phil ignored her, refusing to let his gaze waver from Evelyn. At last the choir director motioned for the other sections to join in. These spies of Greg's could say and do what they wished, Phil thought, but he wasn't going to listen.

"You hide behind a cloak of decency all the while plotting your brother's downfall," the first blonde sang, the words fitting the music perfectly.

Phil's breath caught. He sincerely hoped no one else could hear these ridiculous lyrics.

"The good brother."

"The churchgoer."

"The choir member."

These three lines were sung as solos. The words seemed to linger in the air long after they'd been sung. Phil was convinced everyone knew the taunts were meant for him. Angry and embarrassed, he was about to get down off the riser and escape when he noticed the blonde beside him had vanished. He looked toward the row of first sopranos and saw that the other one was gone, as well. He'd never even seen where the third one had stood. How they'd left he didn't know. Didn't care. Good riddance. His relief was almost palpable.

Sandy began to berate him the minute they were in the car. "Your behavior tonight was appalling," she said angrily. "What's wrong with you?"

"Nothing." The car engine roared to life and he drove out of the church parking lot, eager to put the entire episode behind him.

"Telling Evelyn to shut up was probably the rudest thing you've ever done."

"I wasn't talking to Evelyn."

"If not Evelyn, then who?"

Phil exhaled sharply. "The blonde."

Sandy was quiet for a long moment—unfortunately not long enough to suit Phil. "What blonde?"

"The one standing in front of me. Actually, there were two blondes. No, three, only I didn't see the third, only heard her."

Once more his wife grew quiet. "Phil, there wasn't any blonde standing in front of you," she finally said. "No blonde singing first soprano."

"Yes, there was." He didn't know how Sandy could be so blind. Did she honestly think he'd make up something like this? "Greg sent them."

"*Greg?* Your brother?"

"Who else would do anything so underhanded?"

Silence again. Sandy didn't seem to believe him, which irritated Phil even more. Of course Greg was behind this. He'd put those women up to mocking him in front of his wife and all these other people— and then disappearing. This was exactly the type of stunt his brother would pull, but Phil wasn't going to stand for it. Oh, no. If Greg was planning to make trouble for him, he'd be ready.

"What does Greg have to do with any of this?" Sandy asked.

"He's paid them to spy on me."

"Oh, Phil, that's crazy."

"They had to be spies to know the things they did. Only someone who's been watching me would know I have Greg's loan application on my desk. Furthermore these women seemed to know how much I'm looking forward to turning him down." He hadn't meant to say all of that, but it was too late now.

"You're rejecting Greg's loan application." The accusation in his wife's voice stung.

"He's a bad credit risk."

"Phil, this is your *brother*."

"My selfish arrogant brother." Apparently his wife needed to be reminded of that. "Even at the end of her life, Mom was making excuses for him. Don't *you* start."

"You're jealous, aren't you? Both your parents are long dead, and you still think they loved your brother more than you."

"They did." It was a fact he'd lived with his entire life.

"Greg has come to you looking for help. It couldn't have been easy for him."

"It's not going to get any easier, either," Phil snapped.

"You sound…happy about it."

Phil entered the ramp leading to the freeway with a burst of speed, pushing the accelerator all the way to the floor.

Sandy waited until they were moving smoothly

along with the traffic. "Greg's your brother," she said again. "And you have the power to help him."

Phil tightened his hands on the steering wheel. "You're beginning to sound just like those blondes, singing their solos, humiliating me in front of everyone."

"The blondes sang?" Sandy sounded worried.

"You mean to say you didn't *hear* them, either?"

"No," Sandy said. "Should I have?"

"Yes…no." Maybe it wasn't as bad as he'd first thought. "You're not just saying that, are you?"

"Saying what?"

"That you didn't hear them."

"I didn't," Sandy assured him. "But I still want to know what they said."

He sighed. "According to them, I like to think of myself as the good son and I wear a cloak of decency while plotting against my brother. Something like that." Phil checked the speedometer and realized he was speeding. As he slowed the car, he glanced at his wife, only to discover that she was staring intently at him. "Don't tell me my own wife agrees with them!"

Sandy didn't answer, but her silence said it all.

"Go ahead and be angry," he said, and noted he was speeding again. He seemed in an all-fired hurry to get home and he wasn't sure why. If anything, this argument was bound to escalate once they got there.

"I can only imagine how difficult it must have been for Greg to come to Pacific Union," Sandy said not for the first time. "Especially when he knew that you'd be the one who'd ultimately accept or reject his loan application."

Phil refused to dignify her comments with a response.

"Greg is coming to you for help."

Despite himself, Phil snorted with laughter.

"Oh, Phil, how could you?"

"Easy."

Right after Christmas he intended to call Greg into the bank. He'd leave him to wait and wonder during the holidays. When his brother arrived at the bank, Phil would have him escorted into his office. It would be the first time they'd been face-to-face since their mother's funeral.

Then he was going to personally deliver the news.

Ten

Christmas Eve Matthias stopped at the hospital following his grandson's bone-marrow procedure. Gloria had spent the day with Tanner and called to tell Matthias that the transplant had gone well. Tanner was in an aseptic room Matthias couldn't enter. Only Tanner's mother was allowed to visit, and even then the boy was kept behind a protective plastic barrier. Despite that, Matthias couldn't think of anyplace in the world he'd rather celebrate Christmas.

Because of the unknown bone-marrow donor, they actually had something to celebrate. The change in Gloria since the donor had been located was dramatic. The edge of fear was gone from her voice, and color had returned to her cheeks.

"Dad!" Gloria waved to attract his attention when he walked into the hospital lobby.

"Merry Christmas, sweetheart." He kissed her cheek.

"Dad, Tanner's donor is still here. Everything went as expected, but when he stood up to leave, he blacked out and fell against the hospital bed. He's got quite a gash on his head.''

The donor had asked to remain anonymous and had given up today—Christmas Eve—for Tanner's sake. ''I'm sorry to hear that. Is he okay?''

''He's fine. Said he felt foolish for causing all this fuss. He's in the emergency room, waiting for his wife to pick him up now.''

''I'd like to thank him personally,'' Matthias said. ''Do you think he'd mind?'' This stranger, who'd responded to a newspaper article, had given his grandson a second chance at life. The only reward he'd received for his effort had been a cut on the head—and the grateful appreciation of Tanner's family. The least Matthias could do was sit with him until his wife got there.

''Well, I'll go and talk to him.''

''If you don't mind, I'll go up to Tanner again.''

''Good idea,'' Matthias said. He followed the sign that pointed to the emergency room; it led him to a large waiting area. Groups of people were scattered about. A lone man sat in a shadowy corner, his forehead bandaged. That had to be him.

He walked over. ''Hello, I'm Matthias Jamison, Tanner Westley's grandfather, and I—'' Matthias didn't finish. He couldn't finish. All he could do was gape at the man he'd hated for fifteen years.

''Matthias, is that you?''

''Greg?''

In shock, they stared at each other for the better part of a minute.

"You're Tanner's grandfather?" Greg finally asked.

Matthias nodded.

Apparently Greg hadn't known of the connection between him and Tanner. The anger and hatred Matthias had lived with all these years flared back to life, racing through his blood like a shot of adrenaline. But to his surprise, it died a quick and sudden death.

Matthias claimed the chair across from Greg, astonished that he couldn't think of a single word to say.

"That explains it," Greg said, slowly shaking his head.

Matthias had no idea what he was talking about.

"Now I understand why I was a match for Tanner. It's because you and I are second cousins."

"You mean you really didn't know? That Tanner's my grandson?" Matthias had to ask.

Greg smiled wryly. "Not a clue. You're telling me that was Gloria I talked to a few minutes ago? Your Gloria…and Mary's?" As soon as he spoke, he seemed to regret bringing up Mary's name. "She's certainly changed from the little girl who used to race up and down the vineyard rows."

"It's been a long time."

Greg nodded. He splayed his fingers through his hair and winced when he touched the bandaged gash. His hair was almost completely gray now, but it looked good on him. "She isn't the only one who's changed."

"We've both changed," Matthias murmured, and leaned forward to rest his elbows on his knees.

"About Mary," Greg whispered. "I...I was wrong. I've thought of Mary, of you, so often..." He seemed unable to continue.

Emotion blocked Matthias's throat. It'd been so long since he'd cried that when the tears filled his eyes, they burned and stung like acid. Embarrassed, he blinked hard and looked away. "She died fifteen years ago and I still miss her. Doesn't seem right not having Mary."

"Can you forgive me?" Greg's voice was raw with pain.

"The Lord takes away, but He also gives. Mary's gone, but because of you, young Tanner's got a real chance at beating the same cancer that killed his grandmother."

"Mr. Bennett." Tanner's doctor joined them. Judging by the way he was dressed, he was about to leave. Not that Matthias begrudged him that, seeing as it was Christmas Eve. Edward, like everyone else, wanted to be with his family. "I just heard about your accident and I came to tell you how sorry I am."

Matthias, for one, was grateful for the distraction. It gave him a moment to compose himself.

"Not to worry," Greg said, as if the stitches in his head were of little significance. "It'll be healed in no time. Besides, I should've known better than to stand up without the nurse there."

"I did warn you not to be in too much of a hurry." The doctor smiled, then glanced at Matthias. "I see you two have met."

"We're old friends."

"Cousins, actually," Greg added, and because they needed an excuse to laugh they both did.

"I see…" the doctor said. "You have a ride coming for you?" he asked Greg next.

"Yes. My wife will be here any minute."

"If there's anything else I can do for you, don't hesitate to let me know."

"I won't," Greg promised.

Dr. Thorpe nodded. "I probably won't be seeing you again, Mr. Bennett, but I want you to know that I think you did a brave thing. A selfless thing. Thank you." With that he held out his hand. Greg stood and clasped it firmly.

"Thank you," he returned.

Greg slumped back into his chair, eyes on the retreating physician. "He's a fine young man, isn't he?"

Matthias heard a catch in his voice. "One of the best cancer specialists around." Gloria had repeatedly told him of the wonderful caring physician who'd been so good to Tanner and to her.

Greg's gaze lingered on Dr. Thorpe and his expression was oddly pained.

"You okay?" Matthias asked.

Greg's nod was slow in coming. "I will be."

Not understanding, Matthias frowned. "You want to tell me about it?"

"Perhaps someday," Greg mumbled.

The tension was broken by the sound of carolers. "Joy to the World" drifted toward them, the music festive and lively, a dramatic contrast to their current mood.

"Is it close to Christmas?" Greg asked, seemingly unaware.

"It's Christmas Eve," Matthias told him.

Greg's eyes widened with surprise. "I didn't realize..."

The music made for a pleasant background as the two men continued to talk, mostly about Tanner and Gloria. Several minutes later Matthias brought up the subject of the vineyard. "I read about the fan leaf problems in your area."

"It wiped me out," Greg said.

That accounted for his cousin's haggardness and his beleaguered look, Matthias thought.

"A lifetime of work destroyed in a single season," Greg murmured.

"You're replanting of course."

Greg shook his head. "Takes capital, more capital than I can muster."

"Get a loan. That's what banks are for."

"You think I haven't tried?" Greg's voice rose.

"I'm not a poor risk, at least not on paper, but money's tight. Tighter than I realized. Despite everything, I haven't been able to convince a single bank to give me a loan."

"I've been working with Columbia Wines up in Washington. The vines there are stronger, more resilient. Say the word and I can arrange for you to replant with those."

Greg shook his head again. "Hell, I'm sixty. Too damn old to start over now. Lately I've been thinking of selling out completely and hiring on with one of the other wineries."

That wasn't the answer, as Matthias was well aware. "You never could tolerate working for others. You like being your own boss too much. Besides, you're still young. I'm damn near seventy and I don't think of myself as old."

"Well, I can't get the financing."

"What about Phil? He works for a bank, doesn't he? He should be able to help you."

Greg shook his head. "He has as much reason to hate me as you do."

The carolers drew closer, drowning out any chance of further conversation. Matthias could only imagine what had caused such a rift between the two brothers.

Memory told him that Phil had always resented Greg's good looks, his social skills and sense of purpose. Whatever happened had been building for years. Matthias didn't doubt that Greg had played a role—

but Phil had already been holding a grudge. Looking for a reason to justify his resentment.

Then, without warning, Greg rose slowly to his feet, almost as if he was being drawn upward against his will.

Matthias looked up and then he knew.

Phil saw his brother and Matthias at the same time as Greg saw him. His first reaction was shock, followed by unexpected compassion. Greg—head bandaged, features pale and drawn—stood beside Matthias Jamison, of all people.

Hardly conscious of what he was doing, Phil stopped singing. Sandy did, too. Slowly, involuntarily, he separated himself from the band of carolers. Almost before he realized his intent, he stood silently before his brother. They stared at each other, eye to eye.

Neither man spoke. For his part Phil couldn't find the words. This was what he'd wanted, what he'd dreamed about—seeing his brother, his sophisticated suave rich brother, broken and humbled. Greg was certainly humbled, but to his own amazement, Phil experienced no glee at the sight.

He was incapable of speaking. His mind had emptied, but his heart had grown suddenly full. His eyes filled with tears, and he struggled to hold everything inside.

Then, wordlessly, compulsively, the two brothers strained toward each other and hugged.

"What happened?" Phil asked when they broke apart. He was looking at his brother's bandage.

As if he'd forgotten, Greg touched his head. "Nothing much. It's nothing to worry about."

"Matthias," Phil said, glancing toward his cousin, "I didn't know you still lived in California."

"I don't. I came to see my family—and to thank Greg. He was the bone-marrow donor for my grandson."

Greg had voluntarily given his bone marrow? Phil remembered his brother's aversion to needles—the way he'd always fainted in the doctor's office whenever he had to get a shot.

"I…" Clearly Greg was flustered. "I was a match for the boy. Matthias is our dad's cousin, remember?"

Phil nodded.

"How are you?" Matthias asked.

"Good," Phil told him, and the two exchanged hearty handshakes.

"You still work for Pacific Union, don't you?" Matthias asked him.

"Yes." Phil already knew what his cousin was about to ask.

"Can't you help Greg get the financing he needs to replant?"

"How are you going to answer him?" Sandy whispered, slipping her hand into the crook of his arm. Phil was sure the two men hadn't heard. He was reminded of other voices he'd heard that apparently no one else had. *You hide behind a cloak of decency... The good brother...*

"I'll see to it that you get your loan," Phil said, looking directly at Greg. "Drop in after the holidays to sign the paperwork, and I'll arrange for the transfer of funds."

Greg just stared at him. "Phil," he began hesitantly, "you'd do that for me after..." Words failed him.

"It seems we both had a lot of growing up to do."

"Thank you," Greg said, his voice choked and low.

"Greg!" cried a female voice from across the room.

Phil turned and saw a stunningly beautiful woman at least twenty years his brother's junior come racing across the emergency-room waiting area. "Oh, darling, just look at you."

Greg smiled as the woman ran one hand down the side of his face and inspected the damage to his head. "How did this happen? Omigosh, you can't imagine what I thought when the nurse phoned."

Not answering, Greg placed his arm around the woman and turned to Matthias, Phil and Sandy. "This is Tess, my wife," he said matter-of-factly.

"Hello, Tess," Sandy said, and in that warm welcoming way of hers, extended an invitation to Christmas dinner. Matthias and Gloria were included, too; Gloria would be with Tanner for part of the day, but Matthias thought she could join them for a few hours.

"Can we, darling?" Tess opened her eyes wide. "You know how much I hate to cook. Besides, it's time I met your family, don't you think?"

Greg nodded, still smiling.

The women started talking, and soon it was impossible to get a word in, but Phil didn't mind. And from the looks of it, neither did Greg or Matthias.

"Isn't that the most incredible sight you've ever seen?" Goodness said from her perch atop the hospital light fixture. Shirley and Mercy sat with her, nudging each other as they jostled for space.

Seeing Greg with his brother, his cousin and his wife was heady stuff, indeed. Shirley couldn't have wished for more. Despite their antics, everything had worked out beautifully, and this hadn't been an easy case. Gabriel had made sure of that.

"I see you three are mighty pleased with yourselves," the archangel said as he appeared beside them.

"We did it," Mercy told him with more than a hint of pride.

"And all without involving the FBI or the National Guard," Goodness was pleased to report.

"There was that one minor incident with a hot-air

balloon, though,'' Gabriel reminded her. ''The Federal Aviation Administration is still looking into it.''

Shirley noticed that her friends had suddenly gone quiet. ''All in all, it's been a challenge.'' They'd brought the case to a successful conclusion, but Shirley was convinced it had taken more than a little heavenly intervention. ''What's going to happen to Greg?'' she asked, curious to learn what the future held for the man she'd once thought of as despicable. In time she'd actually come to like him and wish him well. He wasn't as bad as he'd seemed at first glance, and she wondered if this was the real lesson Gabriel had been hoping to teach them.

''Well, as you can see he's mending fences with Tess,'' Gabriel said. Greg had his arm around his wife as they stood and talked to Matthias, Phil and Sandy.

''So their settlement meeting went well,'' Shirley murmured.

''Really well,'' Mercy said, grinning widely. ''Okay, okay, so I joined them for a few minutes. Trust me, the meeting went better than either of them expected.''

''They're getting back together,'' Gabriel continued, ''and are determined to make a real effort to give their marriage another chance.''

''Do they last?''

''With ups and downs over the next few years, but they always manage to work things out. They both decide that love, like most everything else in life, is a decision and they've decided to stay together."

"What about the winery?" Shirley asked.

"Greg does replant with the vines Matthias sells him, and in a few years Bennett Wines will once again be known as some of the area's best."

"Matthias and his grandson?"

"The boy makes a full recovery and Matthias takes frequent trips to California. When the grapes mature, Greg gives Matthias a percentage of the profits as a means of thanking him for his forgiveness and for his help through the early years. That small percentage is enough for Matthias to retire completely. And Gloria meets a good man, a new assistant winemaker hired by Greg. They eventually get married."

"I'm glad," Mercy said. "For all of them."

"What about Greg and Edward?" Goodness asked. "Does he ever find out that Greg's his biological father?"

Gabriel shook his head. "Edward doesn't change his mind about not wanting to know him, and Greg respects his decision. However, he is deeply grateful for the opportunity to have met the son he fathered."

Mercy smiled sadly as the carolers began singing "What Child Is This?" Shirley nodded in understanding.

"Now, are you three ready to return to heaven?" Gabriel asked.

Goodness and Mercy agreed, but with obvious reluctance.

"Can we come back next year?" Goodness asked as they drifted upward.

"We'll have to wait and see," Gabriel told her.

"Yes." Shirley linked hands with her two friends. "We'll just have to see who needs our help most," she whispered to Goodness and Mercy.

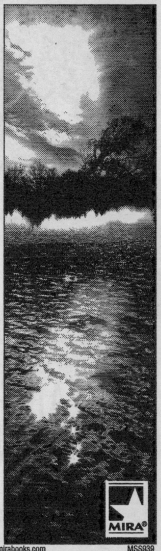

DEBBIE MACOMBER

66891	THURSDAYS AT EIGHT	___ $7.50 U.S.	___ $8.99 CAN.
66830	16 LIGHTHOUSE ROAD	___ $6.99 U.S.	___ $8.50 CAN.
66800	ALWAYS DAKOTA	___ $6.99 U.S.	___ $8.50 CAN.
66602	DAKOTA HOME	___ $6.99 U.S.	___ $8.50 CAN.
66576	DAKOTA BORN	___ $6.99 U.S.	___ $8.50 CAN.
66308	ORCHARD VALLEY	___ $5.99 U.S.	___ $6.99 CAN.
66502	PROMISE, TEXAS	___ $6.99 U.S.	___ $7.99 CAN
66533	MOON OVER WATER	___ $6.99 U.S.	___ $7.99 CAN.
66434	MONTANA	___ $6.99 U.S.	___ $7.99 CAN.
66449	THAT SUMMER PLACE	___ $6.99 U.S.	___ $7.99 CAN.
66260	THIS MATTER OF MARRIAGE	___ $6.99 U.S.	___ $7.99 CAN.

(limited quantities available)

TOTAL AMOUNT $_____
POSTAGE & HANDLING $_____
($1.00 for one book; 50¢ for each additional)
APPLICABLE TAXES* $_____
TOTAL PAYABLE $_____
(check or money order—please do not send cash)

To order, complete this form and send it, along with a check or money order for the total above, payable to MIRA® Books, to: **In the U.S.:** 3010 Walden Avenue, P.O. Box 9077, Buffalo, NY 14269-9077; **In Canada:** P.O. Box 636, Fort Erie, Ontario, L2A 5X3.

Name:_____
Address:_____ City:_____
State/Prov.:_____ Zip/Postal Code:_____
Account Number (if applicable):_____
075 CSAS

*New York residents remit applicable sales taxes.
  Canadian residents remit applicable
  GST and provincial taxes.

Visit us at www.mirabooks.com

MDM1102BL

Christmas 2002

Dear Friends,

As an author I can tell you that some stories are a gift. They arrive in the imagination whole and complete and practically write themselves. It's rare, and when it occurs, I accept it with a prayer of thanksgiving. The book you're holding is that kind of gift. These stories were originally published in 1998 and 1999 under the titles of *Can This Be Christmas?* and *Shirley, Goodness and Mercy*.

Can This Be Christmas? is about a group of passengers, all strangers to each other, trapped in an East Coast train depot on Christmas Eve, and *Shirley, Goodness and Mercy* are my three irrepressible angels.

The idea for *Can This Be Christmas?* was based on my parents' experience when they were caught in a snowstorm in the town of North Bend, Washington. They'd come for Christmas to be with my family. On their way home, Snoqualmie Pass was closed due to the danger of avalanches. I was fifty miles away and unable to get to them. Because my mom and dad are older, I paced and worried, worried and paced. That night, once the storm lessened and the electricity returned, I put on the local evening news—just in time to see an item about the stranded Christmas travelers. The TV coverage showed my dad playing pinochle and my mother helping in the kitchen. Both appeared to be in good spirits, cheerful and upbeat about their circumstances. They made friends during those two days and have stayed in contact with them ever since. Who would've thought...?

As for *Shirley, Goodness and Mercy*—well, they just landed in my lap. This short novel was a return engagement for these three angels—although I hadn't expected to hear from them again! They're Christmas angels who had missions to fulfill, stories to tell and a writer who was willing to do their bidding. It was a match made in heaven (so to speak).

I hope you enjoy both of these stories. I'd also like to suggest that you look around. It isn't only writers who are offered gifts; you just might stumble upon a gift of your own. A gift to last.

Happy holidays,

Debbie Macomber

P.S. I love to hear from readers. You can reach me at P.O. Box 1458, Port Orchard, WA 98366 or through my Web site at www.debbiemacomber.com.